FALLING FOR THE DELTA

SUSAN STOKER
RILEY EDWARDS

Linda —

enjoy!

Susan Stoker

Riley Edwards

ABOUT THE BOOK

When Delta operatives Dash and Magic officially meet Holly and Stella—the women they've had their eyes on—it's hardly a conventional moment, but the fireworks are undeniable. Both men fall hard, fast, and deep, each planning a Valentine's Day their women will never forget. And they don't...but for reasons no one saw coming.

NOTE FROM THE AUTHORS

Hello Reader!

These stories are a collaboration that we came up with one day while we were chatting on the phone. We wanted the stories to "fit" together, and the best way to do that was to have 2 guys and 2 best friend females. We also wanted to write about military Heroes so we decided that writing Delta Force guys was perfect!

Riley's the funny one of the two of us, and she thought up the perfect opening for both the stories. We wanted our heroines to be smart, independent, secure in their sexuality, but not opposed to accepting a helping hand when needed.

And thus our stories were born! They were included in a Valentine's anthology, but we included some extra "sexy times" for this individually published book as well as extra epilogues.

We hope you enjoy reading these fun little stories as much as we liked writing them.

~Riley & Susan

HOLLY & DASH

by Susan Stoker

BLURB FOR HOLLY & DASH

The second they spot each other at Fort Hood, Dash and Holly's happy ever after seems destined. While they didn't exactly meet in a, um...conventional way, there's no denying the fireworks from that fateful moment. Fireworks so hot, Holly suspects their first Valentine's Day together will be one to remember. And it is—but not in a way either is expecting.

HOLLY & DASH

CHAPTER 1

"STELLA!" Holly snapped, trying to get her best friend's attention. But Stella was far too focused on climbing the stupid tree next to her neighbor's balcony.

Stella and Holly had clicked the first time they'd met at their job on Fort Hood Army base in Texas. They'd both just been hired and had been going through new employee orientation. One of the presenters had said something stupid, Holly couldn't remember what it was now, but when Stella had turned to her and opened both eyes wide as if to say, "Oh my God, was that a stupid thing to say," Holly knew she was someone she wanted to get to know better.

And now, five years later, they were closer than

ever—even if at first glance they seemed to be complete opposites.

Holly was short whereas Stella was tall. Holly had dark hair, Stella light. Holly was more reserved, while Stella was outgoing and not afraid to try new things... like climb a tree to get onto her neighbor's balcony so she could climb over the railing and break into her own apartment.

And not just any neighbor either. The hot-as-hell Delta force operative she'd been crushing on for ages. The day he'd moved in, Stella had texted Holly and given her a blow by blow of what was happening. As hard as Stella had worked to try to finagle a way to run into him by "accident," their schedules just seemed too different to have a more casual passing-in-the-parking-lot kind of interaction.

It figured that today of all days, when Stella had locked herself out, Stella's apartment manager was out of town and her friend had already borrowed the extra key she'd given to Holly for situations exactly like this one. A key that was currently locked inside her apartment, along with the one Stella had forgotten.

But like usual, Stella wasn't going to let a little thing like not having a key slow her down. Stella swore the door to her balcony was unlocked and all it would take to get inside was her getting up there.

On one hand, they were both thrilled it was an unseasonably warm day for Texas in January. Stella had on shorts, as it was a weekend and she took every opportunity to wear casual clothes when they didn't have to work. But on the other hand, shorts weren't exactly great for tree-climbing.

"We have a problem," Holly told Stella as she stood under her, attempting to balance with her friend on her shoulders. Holly had no idea what Stella thought she was going to do if she actually fell. There was no way she could actually catch her, but just staring up at her felt wrong. So after Stella actually got hold of the branch, Holly hovered under her like a nervous mother.

But they definitely had another problem at the moment. More than Stella's shirt getting snagged on a branch and her flashing the entire neighborhood when she'd first attempted to shimmy up the tree.

"We don't have a problem," Stella grunted as she did her best to reach upward toward the thicker branch above her head. She had her legs and arms wrapped around the lower branch like a monkey. She hung there for a moment, then exclaimed, "I almost have it!"

"I told you to give me your spare key back," Holly complained.

"Whoop-whoop, I got it!" Stella crowed.

Deep laughter sounded from behind Holly, and she turned to look again at the two men she'd seen approaching. She'd tried to warn Stella that they were no longer alone, but as usual, her friend was completely focused on the task at hand and oblivious to what was going on around her.

"Girl, you need a throat lozenge," Stella said, apparently thinking the men's laughter came from Holly, as she began to shimmy hand over hand across the branch that led right to her neighbor's balcony.

"Abort mission!" Holly said.

"Are you crazy? I'm almost there!"

Holly gave up trying to warn her friend. How Holly always seemed to find herself in embarrassing situations like this when she was around Stella, she didn't know.

When the two men laughed again, Stella finally turned to look down. She froze mid-swing and hung from the tree branch halfway to her goal. "Why didn't you tell me?" she hissed.

"I told you we had a problem," Holly insisted.

Stella began to mumble under her breath, something about the scrapes she'd gotten on her knees and tearing her shirt, but all of Holly's attention was on the two men.

Figured it was none other than the sexy neighbor and his equally gorgeous friend. Why couldn't it have been the maintenance man—the guy with the huge paunch and who smelled like bacon all the time?

Holly hadn't really admitted to Stella that she was interested in her neighbor's friend. If she had, her friend would've been relentless in trying to set them up. For some reason, Stella felt it was her goal in life to get Holly a boyfriend.

So Holly had admired the other man from afar. It seemed as if she saw him all over post too. They apparently liked to eat lunch at the same place in the PX, a small sub kiosk inside the lobby of the post exchange building. She'd smiled at him a few times but had never worked up the nerve to actually talk to him.

And now, here he was, laughing at them.

"Are you open to suggestions?" Stella's neighbor asked, but Holly couldn't take her eyes off his friend. He was tall, but not too tall. Muscular, of course. Had brown hair that was longer than most soldiers were allowed, most likely because he was a special forces operative. His hazel eyes were locked on hers, which made Holly's heart speed up until she was afraid she was going to have a heart attack.

Her attention was jerked back to Stella when she screeched. But her neighbor stepped forward and caught her friend before she hit the ground. It was like a scene from one of the romance books she loved to read.

"Gotcha," he said in a deep, rumbly voice. "You're bleeding," he added.

"Yeah, that happened when she said she knew how to climb a tree. Obviously, she's not very good at it," Holly explained helpfully. It felt better when she concentrated on her friend and tried to ignore the handsome man now standing next to her.

"Let's get you upstairs and get your knees cleaned up," Stella's neighbor said.

"She's locked out," Holly blurted. Stella turned and gave her a shut-up face. In return, Holly widened her eyes and gave her a small headshake.

Both men chuckled once more.

"Come on, Lucy and Ethel, we'll go to *my* place then and get you cleaned up."

"Um, I'm Stella, and she's Holly," Stella told the man holding her.

Holly rolled her eyes and turned to the man's friend. "She's actually brilliant. I know it's hard to tell by her cockamamie idea to trespass on your friend's balcony so she could jump over to hers, but she knows five languages and her IQ is only a few numbers shy of genius. But you know what they say about smart people—many times they lack common sense. And apparently, they don't get classic TV references either."

The look in the man's eyes made her heart rate pick up once more. She felt off-kilter and extremely nervous. He smiled and chuckled, and it was all Holly could do not to throw herself at the man and beg him to be her boyfriend. Some impression *that* would make.

"I'm Dash," he said, stepping closer.

"I'm Holly. Holly Culver." She took the hand he'd extended and her entire body tingled when she felt his warm palm engulf her own.

She vaguely heard Stella's neighbor introduce himself as Magic, but Holly's attention was glued to Dash. He hadn't let go of her hand, and suddenly she felt awkward. Should she pull back? Was this weird? This was definitely weird.

But he didn't give her a chance to comment, or do anything really, before his friend was striding across the lawn toward the apartment complex.

"Um, I should go make sure she's all right," Holly said.

"Magic's got her," Dash said. "I give you my word that he won't hurt her. You live here?"

Holly's mind was spinning. It didn't help that Dash still hadn't let go of her hand. "No. Stella picked me up and we went out for lunch. She was going to drop me off later."

"I'll take you home."

It wasn't a question, and before Holly could respond, he'd shifted, moving the hand that had been holding hers to the small of her back and propelling her toward the parking lot.

Holly knew she should protest. This was how people got kidnapped and killed. But this was the man she'd been secretly crushing on for weeks. And she knew he was a Delta Force operative. She was ninety-nine-point-nine percent sure he wasn't going to drive her to some deserted wheat field and rape and murder her.

But she still turned and looked back at Stella and Magic. She caught her friend's eye and raised a hand up and mimicked talking on a telephone. *Call me later*, she mouthed.

Stella gave her a thumb's up behind Magic's back, then rested her head back on his shoulder.

A deep chuckle sounded from next to her once more, and Holly looked up at Dash.

"If it makes you feel better, you can text her my license plate number. But, Holly, you're safe with me."

And just like that, Holly knew she was a goner. His low, earnest voice, along with the sincerity in his gaze, almost had her melting into a pile of goo right there on the sidewalk. It was stupid—she didn't know this man, but everything within her was telling her he was one of the good guys. That he wouldn't ever hurt her.

She let him guide her to his car, a black Dodge Dart, and she couldn't stop smiling as he opened the door for her. Once she was settled, he stood there for a second looking down at her.

"What?" she asked, nervously pushing a lock of hair behind her ear.

"Nothing. It's just that I can't believe you're here. Finally."

And with that, he shut the door and began to walk around to the driver's side.

Holly had no idea what that meant, but it had to be good, right? Could he possibly have noticed her too and been interested? No, that couldn't be what he meant.

But the spark that had been lit when she'd touched his hand the first time flared inside her. She had no idea what was happening, but she took a deep breath and told herself to not do anything embarrassing. If there was even the slightest chance Dash might be interested in her, she didn't want to do anything to mess that up.

CHAPTER 2

DASH COULDN'T KEEP the smile off his face as he followed Holly's directions to her apartment. The first time he'd seen her at the PX on Fort Hood, he'd been interested, though he wasn't sure why. Maybe it was her quiet confidence. Maybe her feminine shape, which he couldn't take his eyes off of. Whatever it was, she just seemed to exude something that drew him in.

He knew that was crazy. Love at first sight didn't exist. But he couldn't deny there was something about Holly that had definitely gotten to him.

On the day he'd first seen her, she'd seemed oblivious to her surroundings as she'd stood in front of the sub shop and contemplated the menu. Her long black hair had been up in a messy bun and her clothes were professional, yet comfortable. No high heels, no tight skirt. She was petite, probably about half a foot shorter than he was, and round in all the right places.

Dash had worked with many sizes and shapes of women in his lifetime, but there was just something about a woman who had soft curves that drew him like a moth to a flame. Her belly was slightly rounded and her breasts were more than a handful. Her thighs were thick, and he had a brief thought about how they'd feel around his hips.

He'd immediately felt ashamed; it wasn't fair to her to think that way when he didn't even know her.

As he'd stood there daydreaming about her, she'd gotten her sub and walked out the opposite door. Dash had thought he'd missed his chance, but the next day, he saw her again when he was walking from one building to the next.

She obviously worked on the Army post and, from that day on, he seemed to see her all the time. He was still working his way up to actually talking to her when he'd taken his friend, Magic, home that afternoon.

Neither could believe their eyes when they'd walked toward the complex and saw the scene in front of them. Magic had told him all about this gorgeous woman who lived next door to him, and

Dash couldn't deny the tall blonde was a knockout. But he only had eyes for the mysterious woman he'd seen on post.

Holly.

He hadn't needed to consult with Magic about their plan. They'd worked together long enough on their Delta Force team to know what the other was thinking. Magic would take care of Stella and Dash would finally get his chance to get to know Holly better.

"So...is Dash your name or a nickname?" Holly asked.

"Both," Dash admitted.

"That's...unusual, isn't it?" she asked. "I mean, Army guys love nicknames, and especially soldiers on the teams."

"On the teams?" Dash asked, needing to know what information she had about Delta before he said anything.

"Oh, um...yeah. So, here's the thing, I have a top-secret clearance. Stella and I are linguists. We're civilian contractors, but because I'm fluent in Pashto and Arabic, I'm privy to a lot of what's going on over-seas. I translate secret communications between the Taliban and their supporters. Emails and phone calls, that sort of thing. I've met a few Delta teams when they had questions about my translations. And now that I know your name...I know you're Delta. I saw your name on a list of personnel. But I won't say anything. I mean, I could lose my job and get in deep shit, but...yeah."

Dash didn't mind that Holly knew he was special forces. It made things easier for him. "Impressive," he said. And it was. "Thank you for all that you do."

She shrugged. "I don't do much. I sit in my cubicle and stare at a computer all day," she said. "You and your team do the hard stuff."

"Which we couldn't do without intel...so thank you for helping make our jobs safer."

Dash saw Holly blush, and it only made her more attractive. Since it was obvious talking about her job made her uncomfortable, he moved on. "So, my name really is Dash. I don't know what my parents were thinking, but it was easier to yell at me using my first name than my last in basic training."

Holly smiled.

"I take it by that smile that you agree," Dash said.

"I don't remember exactly what your last name is, but I do remember it was long," she admitted.

"Anagnostopoulos," Dash told her.

Holly chuckled and the sound went all the way through him, making his toes curl.

"Yeah, I can't see a drill sergeant yelling that. Dash was obviously much easier for them."

"Yup," he agreed. He wished he could think of something else to say that would make her laugh. He had a feeling it was going to be his mission in life to get her to giggle just so he could hear it.

As he wracked his brain for something else to talk about, he neared her apartment complex. He pulled into the lot, hating that their time together was already over. He hadn't gotten to know her nearly well enough. He longed for more information.

He pulled into a space, turned off the engine, and turned to her. He opened his mouth to ask her something, but Holly spoke first.

"So, what's your story, Dash? Why'd you want to join the Army?"

Loving that she seemed to want to prolong their time together as much as he did, Dash was more than happy to tell her about himself. He told her about his close-knit family and about the worst day in his life, when his father had a heart attack and passed away. He talked about his sisters and how strong his mom was. The story of him joining the Army was a little embarrassing, as he hadn't really planned on it, but when his grades in college were terrible, he decided there had to be more to life than partying and sitting in classes he had absolutely no interest in.

Dash knew he'd been talking way too long and eventually turned the conversation back to Holly. He yearned to learn every little scrap of information about her that he could. He found out that she was thirty-three years old—only two years younger than he was—had grown up in Maryland, had one brother, and her parents were divorced.

But it was when he asked her about how she'd learned Pashto and Arabic that he fell hard and fast for her.

"I was in the fifth grade and a new girl joined our class. She was from Egypt. I felt awful for her because she was extremely shy and didn't speak much English at all. She went to an ESL class in the afternoons, but in the mornings, she just sat at her desk and wouldn't meet anyone's gaze. So I started teaching myself Arabic so I could at least say hello to her. The rest, I guess you could say, is history."

"Wow," Dash said. "That's amazing."

"It's not really," Holly said with a shrug.

"Let me guess, you still keep in touch with her," Dash said with a smile.

Holly stared at him for a long moment before nodding. "I was one of her bridesmaids for her wedding a few years ago."

Dash wasn't surprised. Holly seemed like the kind

of woman who, once you became her friend, you didn't ever want to lose.

"Anyway, I realized that I had an affinity for languages. Spanish and other languages that used a Latin-based alphabet weren't a big enough challenge for me, so I stuck with Arabic and added Pashto for fun." She chuckled. "I know, I'm a nerd."

"I don't think you're a nerd," Dash said in a low voice.

She stared at him with wide eyes from the seat next to him. They hadn't gotten out of the car since he'd parked, and as the sun was setting, he realized they'd been there quite a while getting to know each other.

They stared at each other for a highly charged moment...before Holly licked her lips.

That was it. Dash couldn't stop himself from leaning toward her. The way she started to meet him halfway registered in his brain, giving him the satisfaction of knowing she seemed to be as into him as he was her—then someone rapped loudly on the window next to him.

Dash registered Holly squeaking in surprise but he was already turning and had his hand on the knife he kept strapped near his seat, just in case.

It took him only seconds to realize the man standing at his door was a police officer.

"Open the door," the officer ordered.

Moving slowly so as not to alarm the policeman, Dash reached for the door handle.

"Dash?"

"It's okay, Holly," he reassured her.

He opened his door and stood, making sure to keep his hands where the officer could see them. "Is there a problem?"

"You tell me," the officer said. "We had a report of suspicious activity going on in the parking lot."

"My friend and I have just been talking. That's it," Dash told him.

It was obvious the man didn't believe him. "There have been increased reports of drug activity in this area," the cop said. "Do you have a problem with me searching your vehicle?"

Dash was irritated. This wasn't how he envisioned the evening going. But since he had nothing to hide, he simply said, "No."

After the officer searched him for illegal weapons or drugs and found nothing, he got Holly out of the car and searched her too. By now, two more police cars had arrived.

"Dash?" Holly asked.

"Come 'ere," he told her, holding out an arm.

Without hesitation, she snuggled into his side. Dash loved having her against him, but he hated the circumstance. He held her as the officers did their best to uncover something illegal in his vehicle.

Holly shivered, and Dash mentally swore. The day had been fairly warm for this part of Texas in January, but now that the sun had set, the chilly air had moved in.

"There's a sweatshirt in my backseat," he called out. "My girl's cold, can someone please get it for me?"

He hadn't hesitated to call Holly his girl and hoped she didn't mind. She definitely wasn't a girl, but the phrase had simply popped out of his mouth without him thinking about it.

"I'm okay," she said softly next to him. "You're very warm."

"You're shivering," he said, reaching for the sweatshirt one of the officers brought over to him. "Step back a second," he ordered.

Holly smiled and took a step away from him. Dash hated to let her go for the few seconds it took to help get the huge Army sweatshirt over her head. It was overly large on her slight frame, but Dash had never seen anything as sexy as Holly in his clothes. Visions of her wearing one of his t-shirts—and only his shirt, her long, shapely legs sticking out from under it—flashed through his brain.

"Do I want to know what that thought was?"

Holly asked with a grin as she curled into him once more. One arm went around his back and the other around his stomach. They stood in each other's embrace as if they'd done it every day of their lives. It felt comfortable...right.

"I don't want to say anything that would make you not want to see me again," Dash admitted.

"I don't think that's possible," Holly muttered.

Dash grinned. He leaned down and rested his chin on the top of her head. Once again he marveled at how well they fit together. He opened his mouth to ask if she was feeling warmer when the original officer who'd knocked on his window strolled up.

"Looks like you're good to go."

Dash wanted to roll his eyes, but he merely nodded.

"I suggest if you want to have a chat with your date, that you do so somewhere other than your car in a parking lot."

"Yes, sir," he said respectfully. As annoyed as he was by someone calling the cops on them and having his car searched, he supposed he was glad someone was paying attention, since this was where Holly lived.

"You two have a good night," the officer said before turning and heading back toward his cruiser.

"Well, that was interesting," Holly said, not

letting go of him now that the police had left. "You sure do know how to show a girl a good time."

"This? This was nothing. How about if I pick you up tomorrow and take you on a real date?" The words popped out of his mouth without Dash even thinking about what he was going to say. He held his breath waiting for Holly's response.

She tilted her head up and met his gaze. "You're asking me out? On a date?"

He hated the disbelief in her tone. Did she not know how amazing she was? How the hell she hadn't been snatched up before now was beyond Dash. But other men had officially lost their chance. Their loss was his gain. Now that he'd found Holly, he was going to do whatever he had to in order to keep her. He'd treat her like gold...if only she gave him the chance.

"Yeah, I'm asking you out," he told her.

"Yes," she whispered.

Neither moved. Dash could feel her breathing increase as they stared at each other. He slowly brought a hand up to her face and brushed the backs of his fingers against her cheek. Her skin was smooth, if not a little chilled. She was cold, and as much as he hated to say goodbye, he needed to get her inside. But not before he had a taste of the lips he'd been thinking about since they'd been interrupted earlier.

"I'd like to kiss you," he said. It was a statement and a question all in one.

"Yes, please," she said politely.

Dash's lips quirked upward even as his head was tipping toward her. He felt her go up on her tiptoes as she tilted her head back.

Tingles shot through his body as their lips met, making him feel energized and jumpy. It was as if the universe were sending him a sign that this was the woman made just for him, and making sure he knew it.

Their kiss was chaste at first. Each tasting the other, feeling each other out. Then Holly moaned, and Dash couldn't hold back anymore. He turned her so her chest was crushed against his and brought a hand up to the back of her neck. Her mouth opened and he accepted the invitation. His tongue plunged inside, and he groaned at the rightness of the moment.

She tasted faintly of the mint she'd eaten earlier, while they'd been talking in his car. Dash knew from now on, any time he smelled or tasted peppermint, he'd remember this moment. The first time he'd tasted his woman.

How long they made out, Dash had no idea, but when he heard a cat-call from someone nearby, he abruptly realized where they were. And as much as he wanted to continue to kiss Holly, this wasn't exactly the best place to do it. He eased back, smiling when she frowned and pressed harder against him. Her hands had moved around his shoulders and her fingers grasped his hair, as if she wanted to haul his lips back down to hers.

"Easy, Hol," he murmured.

Her gaze flew up to his then, and she froze in his arms.

Dash ran a hand down her spine, loving how she seemed to arch into his touch, like a cat would when being petted. "I need to get you inside, you're freezing. I thought since we talked through dinnertime tonight, I'd make it up by taking you to one of my favorite restaurants tomorrow night. Do you eat steak?"

It seemed to take a moment for Holly's brain to reengage, which made Dash feel ten feet tall. But he did his best not to smirk about it, even if he wanted to pound his chest and announce to the world that Holly was his.

"I don't make it for myself, as I'm not the world's greatest cook, but yes, I love a good steak."

"Good. How does me picking you up at six tomorrow night sound? That should give you time to get home from work and change if you want. But don't feel the need to dress up. This is a jeans-and-boots kind of place. It's super laid-back."

"That's fine. But, Dash...tomorrow's Monday."

"And?" he asked, his brows furrowing in confusion.

"I just...you don't want to wait for the weekend? Will you be tired?"

"I absolutely don't want to wait," he told her, smoothing a piece of hair behind her ear. Somehow in the last few minutes, the scrunchie that had been holding her hair back had come out and her long black hair was clinging to his chest as if it had a mind of its own. "I can't wait to get to know you better, and every day that passes is a day lost."

"Wow, um...okay."

"Too much?" he asked, worried he'd moved too fast and was freaking her out.

"No. I just..." Her voice trailed off.

"What? Don't ever be afraid to tell me anything. If you're thinking it, I want to know about it," Dash told her.

"I feel the same way. The connection I feel toward you is..."

"Intense," Dash said, finishing her thought.

"Exactly."

He wanted nothing more than to follow her to her apartment, go inside, and show her exactly how powerful their connection could be, but he took a deep breath instead and reached for one of her hands. "Come on, I'll walk you to your apartment."

Holly nodded and squeezed his hand. He walked her into her building and up to the third floor. He stopped in front of her apartment and watched as she unlocked the deadbolt and the doorknob. Then Holly turned and looked up at him a little shyly.

Not able to help himself, Dash leaned down and kissed her once more. This kiss was gentler than the passionate one they'd shared in the parking lot but no less heartfelt.

He forced himself to pull back and said, "Let me give you my number."

She pulled out her phone from her pocket and within a few seconds, they were programmed into each other's contact list.

"You gonna get a sub for lunch tomorrow?" he couldn't help but ask.

"Probably," Holly said. "I know I should pack my lunch, but going out to lunch gets me away from the office for a while every day. I know myself; if I brought something to eat, I'd probably just eat it at my desk and I'd never take a break."

"Maybe I'll see you at the PX then," Dash said, making a mental note to definitely see her at the post exchange the next day.

Holly smiled. "I'd like that."

"Me too."

Dash felt like he'd never smiled as much as he had tonight. It was a nice change.

The hardest thing he'd ever done was take a step away from her. He vowed the time would come, hopefully soon, when he wouldn't have to leave her at her doorstep. That he'd have the right and the privilege of going inside with her. Or she'd come home with him. Though he had a feeling once he got her inside his small house, he'd never want to let her go.

Moving slow was never something Dash did well. Once he found something he wanted, he went after it with everything he had. Holly was definitely not an exception.

"I'll see you tomorrow," he said.

"Text when you get home?" Holly asked tentatively.

Her concern wrapped itself around his heart. "I will."

"Later."

"Later, Hol," Dash said, then like ripping off a bandage, he turned and strode down the hall. He didn't stop smiling the entire way home. And when he texted her and let her know he'd made it home safely, the grin only widened when he got her reply.

. . .

Holly: I'm glad.

Holly: I have an admission. I've been trying to get up the nerve to talk to you for a while now. And I have to say...the reality of you is even better than the fantasy. See you tomorrow.

Dash couldn't resist sending one more text. There was no way he could let her admission go without reciprocating.

Dash: I hope you're ready for this.

Holly: For what?

Dash: Us.

He watched as three dots appeared on the screen, but then they disappeared. Knowing she was speechless wasn't a turnoff. He liked surprising her. He wanted a lifetime of keeping her on her toes, wondering what he had up his sleeve. Holly Culver had no idea that her life had just changed...for the better. He'd do whatever he could to make sure she was always happy and content.

Life with a military man, a Delta at that, wasn't easy. But he'd bend over backward to make sure she always knew how important she was to him. There might be times she had to come second behind his job, but he never wanted her to think she wasn't always on his mind.

Tomorrow felt like the first day of the rest of his life, and Dash couldn't wait for it to begin.

CHAPTER 3

ALMOST A WEEK LATER, Holly knew she was madly in love with Dash Anagnostopoulos. How could she not be? He was the most attentive man she'd ever dated. He simply made her happy. In the past when she'd started dating someone, it always felt a little awkward. She had to search for discussion topics and thinking about being intimate always made her break out in a cold sweat.

But with Dash, everything seemed easy and natural. They never had a hard time finding something to talk about. They'd seen each other every day since they'd officially met. Hung out at lunch, then went out every night. They constantly talked via text, and one night after he'd dropped her off after dinner, he'd called and they'd talked well into the night.

And the physical stuff was just as natural. Holding

hands, putting her arm around him, touching his hand when they sat at one of the picnic tables outside the PX eating their sandwiches at lunchtime, and even kissing. The more she was around him, the more she *wanted* to be around him. Which was quite the revelation.

Holly had always thought of herself as extremely independent. She and Stella were a lot alike in that sense. They'd thought about rooming together, but decided they liked being on their own too much to share a space with someone else...even a best friend. But Holly didn't feel that way about Dash at all.

Her phone vibrated with a text. It was Saturday night, and she and Stella usually went to a movie, or hung out at one or the other's apartments and had some drinks and relaxed together, but tonight they both had dates with their guys.

Stella: You nervous about tonight?

Holly: A little. It's the first time I'll be hanging out with Dash at his place. Are you nervous?

Stella: Hell no! I've been ready for some Magic in my life since he first moved next door!

· · ·

Holly giggled. She was relieved that Stella and Magic seemed to be clicking just as well as she and Dash. It was crazy that the two best friends were dating two men who were best friends. But it also felt...right.

Holly: Maybe down the line we could double date or something.

Stella: Oh, that's definitely happening! Have fun! Don't do anything I wouldn't do.

Holly: Which leaves me open to just about anything.

Stella: Lol. You know it. Text or call me tomorrow...but not too early. I'm fully expecting to sleep in *wink wink*

Holly: Love you

Stella: Love you too, girl!

Holly admired her friend. She wasn't afraid to go after what she wanted. And she obviously wanted Magic. Holly had no idea where the night would go with her and Dash, but she definitely wouldn't complain if it ended with neither of them wearing any clothes and in his bed.

Blushing at the thought, but feeling her nipples harden as she imagined making love with Dash, Holly smiled. Their relationship was moving at warp speed, but it didn't feel wrong. She'd never been the kind of woman who jumped into bed with a guy just to scratch an itch. She had her fair share of sex toys that she used regularly, but she couldn't deny the thought of sleeping with Dash excited her.

Did she love him? Holly wasn't sure. She cared about him and thought about him all the time. She worried about when and where his next mission might be. She'd also already told her mom about him, which wasn't something she did with any of her casual dates. All indicators were pointing in the direction of this relationship with Dash being the real deal.

Taking a deep breath, Holly did her best to put her worries behind her. For now, she was having a good time. She would take things one day at a time.

———

Two hours later, Holly was sitting next to Dash on his couch in his apartment. She couldn't remember being this relaxed around a guy this soon in their relationship. They'd made dinner together in his kitchen and laughed the entire time. Now they were watching a movie on TV and talking.

"So...Valentine's Day is coming up," Dash said.

Holly blinked in surprise. "Yeah, it is," she said.

"You had good ones in the past?"

"Good Valentine's Days?" Holly clarified.

"Yeah."

"I guess."

"That means they've been pretty lackluster," Dash said.

"I mean, I've gotten flowers and chocolate. The usual stuff," Holly told him.

"Hmmmm."

"Dash, we haven't been dating all that long. I don't expect anything from you. I mean, it's really a day made up to sell cards and crap. As far as I'm concerned, it's just another day."

"Maybe it has been in the past, but no longer. And while I agree that it's become pretty commercialized these days, I have no problem making sure my girl knows how much I care about her on the fourteenth of February every year."

Holly blushed. She reached out and poked Dash in the belly.

He sucked in a breath. "What was that for?" he asked, grabbing her hand and holding on to it so she couldn't poke him again.

"Just making sure you're real," Holly quipped.

"I'm real, all right," Dash said. Then he leaned down and covered her lips with his own.

Holly melted under him, as she did every time he kissed her.

Before she knew it, she was on her back on his couch and Dash was lying over her—not crushing her, but surrounding her with his heat and scent.

They kissed for quite a while, then Holly felt one of his hands slip under her shirt and rest on her belly. She sucked in a breath and he lifted his head. He stared down at her but didn't move his hand from where it was resting on the bare skin of her stomach.

"This okay?" he asked.

And just like that, Holly melted once more. Dash was a gentleman down to his bones. He would no sooner do something that would make her uncomfortable than he would cut in front of a granny in the store to get a better place in line.

"Very okay," she reassured him. She thought he'd go back to kissing her, but he didn't lower his head as his hand moved upward.

It was intense to stare into his eyes as he touched her, but Holly loved it. She saw his eyes dilate as his hand closed around one of her breasts. He squeezed her through her bra, and she felt her nipple harden immediately.

"So damn soft," he murmured. He gently pulled the cup of her bra down and then his calloused palm was touching the tender skin of her breast. Holly couldn't help but arch her back, pressing herself harder into his hand.

"You like that."

It wasn't a question. But Holly answered him anyway. "I like everything about you."

He smiled and finally dipped his head back down to hers.

They kissed as he played with her breast. When he lightly pinched her nipple, she moaned. When he pinched it harder, Holly grunted, her stomach tightened, and she felt a gush of wetness between her legs.

Dash moved, surprising Holly. He got up on his knees, then stood. He grabbed her hand, pulled her off the couch, and towed her down the hall toward his bedroom.

It took a second for Holly's brain to catch up with her legs, but when it did, she smiled. Dash didn't stop until he was standing next to his bed. He pulled her into him, and Holly could feel his hard cock pressing against her belly.

"You need to use the restroom?" he asked.

Holly shook her head.

"Are you sure?"

"I'm sure."

"Because once I get you naked in my bed, I'm not going to let you up to breathe for quite a while."

His words made Holly squirm. "I'm sure," she repeated more firmly.

Dash's hands reached for the hem of her shirt and he slowly lifted. Holly's arms went over her head to help him and before the material had cleared her head, Dash was already reaching behind her for the clasp of her bra.

She sucked in her belly as she stood in front of him in nothing but her jeans. She knew she wasn't exactly toned, but he didn't seem to care. Dash went down on his knees in front of her and nuzzled the pooch she'd never been able to get rid of.

"So fucking beautiful," he murmured against her skin. His breath tickled, but Holly wasn't even close to laughing. His hands reached for the button and zipper of her jeans...and before she knew it, she was standing in front of him without a stitch of clothing on.

He inhaled deeply, and a flash of embarrassment ran through Holly. She knew she was turned on. She could feel the wetness on her inner thighs. But like everything with this man, he immediately put her at ease.

He stood up and motioned to the bed with his chin. "In."

Holly moved to get on the bed as Dash disrobed. By the time she got settled on her back, Dash was climbing onto the mattress. He was absolutely beautiful. Muscles bulged in his arms as he used them to support his weight. His cock was long, thick, and oh so hard. The tip brushed against her thigh as he came over her, smearing a bit of precome on her skin. Holly wanted to touch him, to make him as crazy as he was making her. But he didn't give her a chance.

"You're mine," he growled.

Holly could never picture what the authors in the romance books she liked to read meant when they wrote that a man growled. But after hearing Dash tell her that she was his in that rumbly, low tone, she got it.

"And you're mine," she returned.

"Fuck yeah," Dash agreed. "I'm never letting you go."

Holly's stomach clenched in need. "I'm okay with that."

"You better be," Dash said, then he moved down her body until his face was between her legs.

"Dash?" Holly asked, uncertain. She'd given and received oral sex once or twice but in no way felt used to either, but the intense look on Dash's face gave her pause.

"Shhhh," he said. "Let me make you feel good."

Holly's head flopped back against the pillow, and a waft of Dash's musky scent filled the air around her.

She moaned at the first touch of his tongue and dug her fingernails into his forearms as he began to pleasure her.

She kind of thought Dash would be aggressive, would go at her hard and fast, but she was surprised when he did nothing but gently lick her folds at first. Gradually, her muscles relaxed as she got used to his touch.

"You good?" he asked, lifting his head.

Holly realized he'd purposely gone easy until he felt she was more comfortable.

"Yeah. I'm sorry, this is kinda new for me."

The look of lust and satisfaction on his face was easy to see.

"You're gonna love this," he said.

Holly opened her mouth to respond, but swallowed her words when Dash closed his lips around her clit and sucked.

She jolted in his grasp, but he held her hips tightly as he got to work. It was obvious what he'd done before was simply a warm-up and this was the real deal. When he began to flick his tongue over her clit, Holly couldn't keep the moan from escaping.

"Oh, fuck," she said.

She felt Dash chuckle against her intimate parts. Holly had used her fingers and toys to get herself off, but nothing felt like Dash's lips and tongue. He also wasn't letting her pull back. He was relentless as he worked her clit.

She felt her orgasm rising from deep within her and tried to jerk away. She just needed a small break, but he wouldn't give it to her. In fact, instead of pulling back, he came up on his knees and lifted her hips in the air, giving her even less traction. She couldn't thrust, couldn't pull away. She was at Dash's mercy.

Holly didn't know whether to be overjoyed or freaked out. But Dash didn't give her a chance to do anything but feel. He began to suck even harder, treating her clit like a nipple. He even used his teeth lightly on it, and Holly cried out as pleasure coursed through her.

Her legs began to shake, then her belly. Every muscle in her body tensed as the pleasure washed over her. It wasn't gentle. It was fast and hard, and Holly swore she saw stars as she flew over the edge.

Holly expected Dash to ease up now that she'd come, but he didn't. He kept his mouth glued to her clit and licked even harder.

The second orgasm slammed into her even before the first had ended. Holly's mouth opened and she gasped for breath as the pleasure-pain roared through her overstimulated body. She wasn't sure if she liked this or not, but couldn't deny it was a heady experience.

She was still shaking when Dash finally took his mouth from her clit and lowered her hips.

"Holy shit," she whispered.

But apparently, Dash wasn't done. He got down on his belly once more and gently eased a finger inside her now soaking-wet body.

"Oh my God," he said in a reverent tone. "You're so damn gorgeous. Hot. Wet. Tight. That's it, squeeze my finger like you're gonna do to my cock."

Holly had never particularly enjoyed dirty talk in bed. It always seemed contrived to her. Cheesy. But listening to Dash only turned her on more.

He eased another finger inside her and began to slowly pump them in and out. Lifting her head, Holly saw his complete attention and focus was between her legs. It should've been embarrassing, but instead, it was the most erotic thing she had ever seen.

Then he turned his hand so his palm was facing the ceiling, and he held his hand still as his fingers moved inside her. His other hand moved to rest on her pelvic bone and before she realized his intention, his thumb began to stroke her extremely sensitive clit.

She jerked in his arms and he grunted in satisfaction. Dash licked his lips as he watched her reaction to what he was doing.

"You ever had a G-spot orgasm?" he asked.

It took Holly a moment for his question to register. "Um...I don't think so," she said honestly.

"If you don't know, you haven't. I don't know if this will work, but you're wet enough and I think you've got it in you. Hang on, Hol. This is gonna get intense."

Intense? And what he'd already done hadn't been? Holly opened her mouth to protest, to tell him she wasn't sure about being able to handle any more, but her words died when his fingers inside her began to move again.

He thrust his fingers in and out of her body, brushing against a spot deep inside her that made Holly gasp in surprise.

"That's it. There it is," Dash said with satisfaction.

Holly screeched when his thumb began to flick hard against her clit once more.

Her fingers slammed onto the mattress and she dug her nails in, trying to get purchase. She'd never felt anything like what Dash was doing to her at the moment. Her vision went black and it felt like she had to use the bathroom. For a second, she panicked at the thought of peeing all over Dash.

She'd never recover from the embarrassment if that happened.

"Let go, Holly. I've got you."

And then she couldn't think anymore. Pleasure roared through her body like a freight train. She felt a gush of liquid between her legs and heard Dash's grunt of satisfaction. Holly felt high, like she had that one time she'd tried a joint in high school. It was euphoric and scary at the same time.

When she finally came back to herself, Holly felt Dash gently stroking her thighs and her belly. He was murmuring all kinds of praise for her and telling her how beautiful she was. All Holly could do was lie there and wonder if anyone had ever died from too much pleasure.

In a daze, she watched him finally move back up her body. He rolled a condom over his cock and she held her breath as he lined himself up to her soaking-wet folds.

"You ready?" he asked.

Holly could only nod. Was she ready? She felt as if she were born ready for this man.

He pressed inside her slow and steady and when he was all the way inside, Holly felt claimed. She wrapped her thighs around his hips, dug her fingers into his biceps, and stared into his eyes as he began to make love to her.

It was nothing like anything she'd ever experienced before. This man was hers. Heart and soul.

"Mine," he whispered as he tenderly pressed in and out of her body.

"Yours," Holly agreed.

Dash was beautiful. There was no other word for him. His sculpted naked chest rippled as he held himself over her. She lay under him in a semi-daze. She'd never felt as wrung out as she had after that last orgasm he'd given her, but as he made love to her, amazingly, she began to feel another orgasm building.

"Oh my God, death by orgasms," she blurted.

Dash laughed, and she actually felt his cock twitch deep inside her as he did so. "But what a way to go," he said.

Holly gripped Dash's biceps harder as he moved his hips up and down. She was so wet, he easily slipped in and out of her. She winced at the thought of the wet spot she'd probably left on his mattress.

"What was that thought?" he demanded.

Holly looked up and met his eyes. Normally, she would've made up some lie, but she still felt as if she were in a fog from the earlier orgasms, so she blurted, "I don't want to sleep on the wet spot."

Dash laughed again.

It was a weird feeling, laughing in the middle of

sex. That had certainly never happened before, but Holly had to admit that she loved it.

"Don't worry, you won't have to. I'll change the sheets every morning for the rest of our lives if you gift me with orgasms like you did earlier."

Holly smiled shyly up at him. "That hasn't happened before."

"Good," he said smugly. "You ready for one more?" he asked.

Holly's nipples hardened at the thought, but she shook her head. "No."

"Well, you need to get ready, because I'm not gonna last long. You're too fucking tight. Too good. I'm never gonna get enough of this pussy. It's mine now. Understand?"

His words were crude, but somehow they only turned Holly on more. She nodded.

He fucked her hard then, his eyes straying to her breasts as each thrust made her boobs bounce up and down on her chest.

"You're perfect," Dash murmured. "So fucking beautiful. Every inch."

He was talking more to himself than to her, but Holly loved hearing every word.

Then he shifted, bracing himself on one hand, and went still deep inside her body.

Holly shifted, wanting him to thrust some more. Amazingly, it felt good. Really good.

His free hand brushed her belly as he snaked it between them. Then he began to tweak her clit once more. "Come, Holly. I want to feel you cream all over my cock. I can't wait to take you bare. When I can feel you without anything between us. That's it. Come for me. Once more."

She honestly didn't think she had another orgasm in her, but she was wrong. The feel of being stuffed full with Dash's cock and the expert way he'd learned to flick her clit in the short time he'd known her had her coming in record time. This one wasn't as intense as the others, but it was no less intimate and over-whelming.

Dash's hand slammed against the mattress at her shoulder even before she'd finished shaking, and he was once more fucking her hard and fast.

It was animalistic and carnal, and Holly loved seeing the normally completely in control Dash lose it. He grunted and made noises in the back of his throat, then he clenched his teeth, stared down into her eyes, and held himself still deep inside her body as he finally let himself come.

His legs were shaking, and Holly felt proud that she'd been able to do that.

He fell on her, catching himself at the last minute

so he didn't squash her. He rolled until she was on top. He was still inside her, and Holly knew she'd remember this moment for the rest of her life.

"Thank you," Dash said quietly.

Holly smiled. "I think that's my line," she quipped.

"No, it's definitely mine. I'm keeping you," Dash informed her casually, as if he were telling her the time.

"Okay," Holly said, suddenly exhausted. She only vaguely felt him move her off him and leave the bed. He was back in less than a minute, cuddling up behind her, holding her tight against his chest.

Sighing in contentment, Holly fell into a deep sleep.

———

Holly woke up in the middle of the night and found herself lying on her side, with Dash snuggled tightly behind her. He had one arm around her waist and his breathing was deep and even. The feel of his naked body against her own made goose bumps break out on Holly's arms.

This was everything she'd ever wanted. And the sex was...unbelievable. She'd never understood what all the fuss was about. She got it now.

Without thinking about the fact it was three in the morning and that Stella was probably sound asleep, Holly reached for her phone, which Dash had so generously gone out to the other room to get for her. She hadn't needed it, but he'd insisted it was safer to have a phone close at hand in case something happened in the middle of the night.

She loved how caring and concerned Dash was. He'd been that way all week, constantly asking how she was doing, how she was feeling, if she was working too hard, eating enough, etc.

Holly shared everything with Stella. They'd talked at length at work about Dash and Magic and how crazy-fast their relationships were moving. But both felt comfortable with the speed. Neither had gone all the way with their men before tonight, and Holly couldn't resist following up on a conversation they'd had at work the day before.

Holly: Definitely a 12 on a scale of 1 to 10.

Then she put the phone back on the small table next to the bed, and turned in Dash's arms. He stirred.

"You good?"

"I'm perfect," Holly told him.

"Yes you are," Dash mumbled.

Holly buried her nose into his chest and curled her arms in front of her. Dash's arms tightened around her waist and she could feel his cock twitch against her belly. She smiled. Neither was ready for another round right this moment, but knowing that she could turn him on even when he was half-asleep did wonders for her self-esteem.

"Hol?"

"Yeah?"

"Love you."

Holly froze. Did he just say what she thought he said?

"And no, I'm not talking in my sleep," Dash added. "It's late...or early. Too soon to get up. Go back to sleep," he ordered.

Holly took a deep breath and closed her eyes. She should've been freaking out that he'd said the L-word, but she wasn't. That said a lot about her feelings toward this man.

Right before she fell asleep, she felt Dash kiss the top of her head, then relax once more.

CHAPTER 4

"YOU WANT me to pick up a sandwich for you today?" Holly asked Stella before she headed out the door. It was the day before Valentine's Day and things between her and Dash, and between Stella and Magic, had never been better. It was hard to believe that a month ago they'd been ogling the men from afar and now they were...ogling them from much closer proximities.

"No, I'm good. Magic is coming over and bringing us something. We're gonna go out to the tables between here and the PX and have a picnic."

"You know what he's got planned for tomorrow?" Holly asked.

"No clue, and it's driving me crazy," Stella admitted.

"Yeah, I keep trying to get Dash to give me a hint and he's been extremely secretive about it all."

"Guess that comes from being a Delta, huh?" Stella asked.

"I guess so. All right, I'm headed out. I'll be back in about forty-five minutes or so."

"Sounds good. Dash meeting you at the PX?" Stella asked.

"Of course," Holly said with a smile and a wave.

She walked the three blocks to the post exchange...and for some reason today, she felt as if there was a weird vibe in the air. Holly had no idea why, but she couldn't shake the feeling that something felt...off.

She hated being paranoid but still felt herself walking a little faster. As a result, she arrived at the PX before Dash. She entered the building and headed for the small kiosk that sold the subs she was addicted to.

The building that held the PX was set up sort of like a mall. A large open space was at the front, with a clothing shop for the soldiers on base, a flag shop, a store that sold powder nutritional supplements and other health food, and had several kiosks in the middle of the space that were rented by various small businesses. Large windows lined the outer wall, facing the parking lot, letting in lots of light.

A separate food court was in a building next to the PX, but Holly had always preferred the less crowded sub shop in the PX building partly because it wasn't quite as busy here as in the food court.

"Hey!" said Annabel, the employee who worked most weekdays at the sub kiosk, as Holly approached.

"Hi."

"You want your usual?" Annabel asked.

"Yes, please. And since I'm here, I might as well order Dash's too."

"Extra jalapeños, right?" Annabel asked.

Holly wrinkled her nose. "I don't know why he loves those things so much, but yes."

"You got it."

As Annabel made their sandwiches, Holly stared out the front windows. As she unconsciously searched for Dash, something caught her eye. It was a man. He was wearing camouflage, which wasn't surprising, since they were on an Army base—but it took a second for the object in his hands to register in Holly's consciousness.

It was an automatic rifle.

A moment after that registered in her brain, Holly heard the unmistakable sound of gunshots.

"Holy shit," she muttered.

"What was that?" Annabel asked, turning toward the window.

As she watched, the man turned and headed toward the PX. Holly was moving before she even thought about it.

"Go!" she yelled, running around the small kiosk and grabbing Annabel's arm. "There's a guy out there with a gun! Shooting!"

Just as she said the last word, another volley of gunshots sounded, closer now.

People around them started to panic. Someone screamed.

"Go into the PX!" Holly yelled as she pointed toward the entrance to the store. It was down the large open space to the left. There was an employee looking their way, obviously startled by Holly's shouts.

"Go to the back, away from the windows! Go, go, go!" Holly ordered trying to get the customers milling around the outer area of the store to get to safety.

For whatever reason, people seemed to listen to her. Everyone ran toward the PX entrance as if their lives depended on it...which they probably did.

Holly turned to check on where the man with the gun was once more and was alarmed to see how much ground he'd made in the short time she'd taken her eyes off him.

He was yelling now. In Arabic. His voice was

muffled through the glass, but it was obvious he was delusional, shouting *"Allahu Akbar"* over and over.

He might think his God was the greatest, but Holly couldn't waste any time thinking about what his motives might be, because next, she immediately saw Dash. He was in the parking lot, in the direct path of the crazy man with the gun.

In a few seconds, the shooter was going to walk right past the vehicle Dash was crouched behind—and probably take the opportunity to shoot him.

Then Holly noticed that Dash wasn't alone. He was crouched with a woman and her child, a little girl probably around five years old. The terror on their faces was clear, even from where Holly was standing.

She moved without thinking. If she could get the shooter's attention, make him change direction and come after her, he wouldn't see Dash, or the woman and child.

With adrenaline coursing through her veins, Holly ran faster than she'd ever run in her life to get to the opposite side of the lobby, to the other door. She burst through and turned to see the shooter.

She opened her mouth and yelled in Arabic as loud as she could. "What are you doing? Stop it!"

The man immediately stopped and turned to look at her. An evil smile crossed his face and he changed direction, pointing his rifle at Holly as he walked toward her. He began to speak in Arabic, talking about his mission and Allah once more.

Holly didn't stick around to listen—she bolted back into the lobby in the front of the PX.

Out of the corner of her eye, she saw the mother and little girl running toward the other side of the building. She sighed in relief as they disappeared around the brick structure, safe.

But Dash didn't follow them. Instead, he ran for the door on the other end of the PX lobby.

More gunshots rang out and the glass in one of the huge windowpanes at the front of the building shattered into a million pieces. Holly couldn't help but let out a scream of fright. She ducked and ran toward the other door...and Dash. She had no idea what he was going to do, but just having him there made her feel a hundred times safer.

The look on Dash's face as he slammed through the door made Holly pause for a moment.

This was the soldier. The deadly Delta Force operative.

Then she was in his arms. But it wasn't a loving embrace. His hands were rough as they grabbed her biceps and forced her down into a crouch behind one of the kiosks in the middle of the lobby.

More gunshots rang out, and another window shattered.

"I'm going to kill you, woman. I must kill all infidels!"

"What's he saying?" Dash asked.

Holly told him, then couldn't help but be impressed at the litany of swear words that left his mouth. The man next to her was as different as night and day from the man she'd spent the last couple of weeks sleeping next to. He was hard, deadly. But Holly wasn't scared of him.

How could she be scared of the man she loved?

"On the count of three, we're going to make a run for the entrance to the PX," Dash told her.

Holly shook her head. They wouldn't make it. How she knew that, she wasn't sure. But she knew if they even peeked their heads out from behind their hiding space, they were dead. Dash wasn't armed; why would he be on a random weekday? But that didn't mean he wouldn't do whatever he could to stop the threat. That was just who he was. And Holly couldn't lose him. Not after she'd finally found him.

Time seemed to stop. Holly stared at Dash and tried to let him know without words how much she loved him. She'd never said it out loud, figuring she had plenty of time to tell him later.

Sirens sounded in the distance, and Holly got an idea. She thought about how many people were probably hiding inside the building. The parking lot had been pretty full. If the shooter got inside, there was no telling how many people might be wounded or killed.

"They're coming!" she yelled in Arabic. "You better run!"

It was lame, but she didn't have time to think of anything better to say. She didn't really want the man on the loose on the post, but she definitely didn't want him coming inside the building.

He responded with another volley of shots and another window shattered under the onslaught of bullets. Holly swore she felt a shot go right by her head. Dash pulled her harder into him, and she gladly buried her head against his chest once more. The position was awkward, as they were both crouched on the balls of their feet behind the kiosk, but Holly wanted to be ready to run at a moment's notice, and figured Dash felt the same way.

After a few seconds, to her surprise, Holly heard more gunshots—farther away than they'd been before. And when no more glass broke, she lifted her head and stared at Dash.

"Is he leaving?" she whispered.

Dash nodded. "Stay here," he ordered.

Holly clutched at him for a moment before forcing herself to let go. This was what Dash did. She had to trust he wasn't going to go toe-to-toe with a terrorist while he was unarmed.

He was only gone for a few seconds, but it seemed like an eternity.

"Come on," Dash said, scaring the shit out of Holly when he reappeared next to her. He had his hand out, and Holly took it without hesitation.

"Where'd he go?"

"I'm not sure, but from the direction of the shots, it sounds like he went around the building to the east."

"Toward *my* building?" Holly asked anxiously. "Stella said she was going to have a picnic with Magic! We have to do something."

"What we have to do is stay safe, and make sure everyone inside is safe too," Dash said firmly. "Magic's not going to let anything happen to Stella."

"Promise?" Holly couldn't help but ask.

"Promise. And for the record, I'm pissed at you," Dash added as he led her toward the entrance to the PX.

"At *me*? Why?" Holly asked in surprise.

"Because you put yourself in danger," Dash said between clenched teeth.

"But...he was going to see you!" Holly protested. "He would've shot you for sure."

She watched as Dash's nostrils flared and he took a few deep breaths. Then, right there in the middle of the women's clothing section of the PX, he turned and hauled her into his arms.

The store was eerily quiet, the only sound muffled voices coming from somewhere toward the back of the store.

"I can't lose you," Dash said into her hair and he clutched her to him.

What she'd done, and what had almost happened to Dash, began to finally sink in. She shook as she clung to Dash.

"Shhhh, you're okay. I've got you," he said. "I'm pissed, but also damn proud. You were amazing," he told her.

"I love you," Holly blurted. "I know this is crazy but when I realized he was going to see you and probably shoot you, I just acted."

"Fuck," Dash muttered.

They stood like that for at least a full minute, simply soaking each other in, reassuring themselves that they were both alive and well.

Then Dash pulled back and stared down at her. "You mean it?"

Holly knew what he was talking about. "Yes. I love you."

"And I love you. I don't care how fast it's been. I think I knew from the first time I saw you."

"Hey! You guys all right?" a voice called out.

Dash took a deep breath. "Come on, I need to get moving. See what I can do to help. You'll stay here?"

Holly nodded. "I speak Arabic," she reminded him unnecessarily. "If I'm needed to translate, just text me and I'll come running."

"No way in hell," Dash murmured under his breath.

"Dash," Holly warned, but he shook his head.

"I'm not putting you in danger. No fucking way. If —and this is a big if—they subdue this asshole and need someone to translate, I'll consider it. But while he's walking around with a loaded weapon and shooting people, and after he threatened to kill you, you're not getting anywhere near him. You were already way closer than I'd ever want you to be to a terrorist."

Holly couldn't help but melt at that. "Okay."

"Did you guys hear me? Are you all right?" the PX employee called out again.

"Go. I need to check on Magic."

"Okay." Holly went up on her toes and kissed him hard and fast. "Go do your thing. Love you."

"Love you too."

Then he turned, headed toward the front of the store.

Holly let out a long breath, still shaky on her feet, and walked toward the back of the store and the others who were still hunkered down there.

CHAPTER 5

DASH STILL FELT OFF-KILTER. The day before had been long and extremely stressful.

The man who'd decided to make a murderous statement had been an American Army officer, with distant family members who were Muslim. He claimed his actions were retaliation for the US wars in the Muslim world. He'd ended up killing three people and injuring fourteen. It could've been a lot worse if it hadn't been for some very brave soldiers who'd literally tackled the man and stopped his massacre.

Magic and Stella had been in his direct path as he'd fled from the military police hot on his tail, but luckily neither had been injured.

Holly had taken years off his life when she'd burst

out of the PX and confronted the shooter. She could so easily have been hurt, but he couldn't deny that she'd probably saved both him and the mother and child he'd been with from being injured or killed.

They'd spent the rest of the day talking with the authorities and the evening in each other's arms. Neither could seem to let go of the other. They didn't make love; Dash couldn't even think about passion. All he could think about was how bereft he'd be without her...and that certainly wasn't conducive to making love.

That morning, Valentine's Day, he'd woken up to the feel of Holly between his legs, giving him the best blow job he'd ever received. He'd tried to hold back, but it was no use. She'd insisted on finishing him off with her mouth, but afterward, he'd been sure to reciprocate.

He'd planned a full day of romantic gestures for her, but after yesterday, all he wanted to do was stay holed-up inside his house, keeping her all to himself.

After showering, they had breakfast, and Dash was attempting to muster up the enthusiasm to give Holly the best Valentine's Day she'd ever had, when he spied a worried look on her face.

"What's wrong?" he asked.

"Nothing's wrong, really," she said. "I was just

thinking about today. I know you've planned something elaborate...and I don't want you to think I'm not appreciative of whatever it is."

"But?" Dash asked, walking toward her, not able to keep his hands off her. He pulled her into him, lacing his fingers together at the small of her back. She fiddled with a button on the front of his shirt and wouldn't look at him as she spoke.

"I was just thinking that I'd like to hang out here with you today. Just the two of us. I'm not sure I'm ready to head out into the big bad world so soon after what happened."

Dash sighed in relief. God, she was perfect for him. "Look at me, Hol."

She lifted her chin and met his gaze.

"I was trying to find a way to say the same thing, but I didn't want to let you down after the way I talked up how amazing today was going to be for you."

"You don't need to go out of your way to do stuff for me, Dash. Just being with you is enough."

"I love you," he told her.

Holly smiled. "And I love you."

"You're really okay with staying in?"

"Yes."

New plans began to swirl in Dash's head. "Okay.

We'll hang out here. But I do still want to do something special for you later. I'm going to need you to hang out in our bedroom while I get stuff ready."

"*Our* bedroom?" she asked.

Dash grinned. "As far as I'm concerned, it's ours."

"I like that," Holly said, blushing.

"Me too." Dash couldn't resist leaning down to kiss her. He couldn't seem to keep his hands or lips off her. He could've lost her, and he knew down to the tips of his toes that if that had happened, he wouldn't have recovered.

For the rest of the afternoon, they snuggled together on the couch, watched a rom-com that Holly had said she'd always wanted to see, had lunch. Holly talked to Stella on the phone, he texted Magic, and as the sun was setting, Dash sent Holly in to take a long, relaxing bath while he set the scene in the living room.

Satisfied that he'd done all he could to make the room as romantic as possible, Dash went and got Holly. He made her close her eyes as he led her out into the living room.

"Open them," he told her.

She opened her eyes and gasped. "Holy crap, Dash, it's beautiful!"

Dash smiled. He'd transformed his living room

into a fort of sorts. He'd used sheets and blankets and Christmas lights to make an intimate space complete with pillows, champagne, and even chocolate. It was leftover candy his mom had sent him for Christmas, but it was the only thing he had on hand.

He led Holly inside the fort and smiled at the wonder in her eyes. Dash sat on the floor on the pillows with his back against the couch, and when Holly sat in front of him, he pulled her back against him. She snuggled in and sighed.

"I hope that was a good sigh."

"It was," she reassured him. "No one's ever done anything like this for me before. Thank you."

"I promise to do better next year," Dash said.

"I don't think you can."

Dash grinned. She was wrong. He knew just what he wanted to do next Valentine's...but he had a year to plan.

Thoughts of anything other than the here and now flew from his mind when Holly turned in his embrace and she began to caress his inner thigh. "What did you have in mind for the entertainment portion of the night?" she asked saucily.

"I thought maybe we could take a nap," he teased.

Holly giggled. "Okay, why don't you lie down then? Right here, on your back." She scooted away a bit to give him room and Dash gladly stretched out where she indicated. He put his hands behind his head and grinned up at her.

"I'm here, now what?"

"You sleep. I'm gonna play," Holly said with a glint in her eye. Her hands went to the fastener of his pants, and just like that, Dash was hard.

"I think I might like to play with you."

"I was hoping you'd say that," Holly told him.

The next hour was one of the most erotic and sensual of Dash's life. Making love with a woman you wanted to spend the rest of your life with, and with whom you'd shared a life-and-death experience, was more intense than anything he'd ever experienced before.

They were both sweaty and limp with exhaustion as they lay under the lights and sheets he'd strewn around the room.

"Holly?" he whispered as he held her against him. He was on his back and she was curled up next to him with her head resting on his shoulder.

"Yeah?"

"Happy Valentine's Day."

"You too. I'm sorry my card was so lame compared to all this," she said, gesturing around her.

"I don't need a card. Or a gift. All I need is you."

"I feel the same way," Holly told him.

They fell asleep right there in the living room,

cuddled in each other's arms. It might not have been the Valentine's Day he'd expected a month ago, but Dash wouldn't change anything about this moment. He was a better man because Holly was in his life, and he'd forever be grateful he and Magic had walked up on Holly and Stella's crazy scheme.

EPILOGUE

ONE YEAR Later

"What do you think our guys have planned?" Holly asked Stella. It felt like *déjà vu*

from last year when she'd asked the same thing.

It was Valentine's Day, and Dash had told Holly he had something special planned for her today. Holly had tried to protest, telling him she didn't need any grand gestures, she just wanted to spend time with him, but he'd only smiled.

Then when she'd gotten to work, Stella had said Magic had told her practically the same thing. So now both women were extremely curious.

Looking at her watch, Holly saw that it was four

o'clock. Almost time to leave, thank goodness. It had been a very long day full of anticipation and curiosity.

"I have no idea. But I'm sure whatever they've got cooked up, it'll be awesome," Stella said.

Holly smiled at her best friend. The year had been a good one for both of them. They'd started dating the men they'd had huge crushes on, had moved in with them, and both their relationships were stronger than ever.

The deployments were hard, but Holly had gotten through them with Stella's help. Not to mention the other wives and girlfriends of the men on Magic and Dash's team. Military spouses for the most part really helped each other out. It was like having a second family.

A commotion outside Holly's office caught both women's attention, and they looked at each other with huge grins on their faces. As one, they headed for the doorway to see what was going on, and to discover if their hunch that whatever was happening had to do with their men was correct.

It was.

Walking down the hallway toward them were Magic and Dash. They were both wearing their dress green uniforms and each held a dozen red roses.

Holly turned to look at Stella and saw she had a huge smile on her face, one that matched her own.

Then Dash's gaze caught hers, and Holly couldn't look away. He really was a hell of a gorgeous man. And he was all hers. She had no idea how she'd gotten so lucky, but every day she got to spend with him made her a better person. She'd never been as happy as she'd been over the last year.

When Dash arrived in front of her, he handed her the roses. Holly took them and buried her nose in the bouquet. The smell was divine.

"Hi," she said somewhat lamely. She could hear Magic and Stella talking next to her, but all her attention was on the man she loved.

"Hi," Dash returned and held out his hand.

Without hesitation, Holly put her hand in his. He turned and started walking back down the hall.

Stumbling a bit, Holly said, "Wait, I can't leave yet! It's not five o'clock yet!"

"I've already talked to your boss about leaving early," Dash said calmly as he continued walking. "She had no problem with it."

"But, my purse!" Holly said desperately.

As if her words were some sort of signal, her boss called out from behind them, "I've got it! Here you go, Holly! Have fun!"

Holly took her purse from the other woman and did her best to try to look calm, cool, and collected, when inside she was kind of freaking out. She had no idea where Dash was taking her or what was going on. She wasn't scared—how could she be when she was with Dash?—but still.

Looking back once more, she saw Stella also being towed along by Magic. She widened her eyes at her friend as if to ask, 'What the hell is going on?'

As always, Stella could read her nonverbal signals, and she shrugged. But the huge smile on her face told Holly she was just as excited about whatever was happening as she was.

They walked out of the office, and all four of them got into the elevator.

"Where are we going?" Holly asked.

"You'll see," Dash said mysteriously.

"You're seriously not going to tell us?" Stella huffed.

"Nope," Magic said with a grin.

The elevator stopped on the ground floor and they all got out and headed for the exit.

Once outside, Magic headed toward his car with Stella, and Dash propelled Holly toward his.

"Call me later!" Stella called out as Magic led her away.

"I will!" Holly told her.

Dash stopped abruptly, and Holly literally walked right into him. But of course, he didn't let her fall. He wrapped his arm around her, holding her steady and plastering her to his front. He leaned down and nuzzled the side of her neck. "No calling or texting Stella until tomorrow," he said.

Goose bumps broke out on Holly's arms as he continued to kiss and caress her neck. He knew she was super sensitive there and was obviously trying to drive her crazy.

"And no texting her with your rating of our sex in the middle of the night either," he added.

Holly couldn't help but chuckle. She'd thought he was sleeping the first night they'd made love, when she'd impulsively texted Stella telling her that he was a twelve on a scale of one to ten.

"Can't you give me a hint on where we're going?" she pleaded.

"Nope," Dash said, standing up straight, then grabbing hold of her hand once more and walking toward his car.

"I hope we're not going out, because with you dressed like that...I'm seriously underdressed for any kind of fancy dinner."

"You're beautiful," Dash said. "Perfect exactly how you are."

Holly loved that about her man. He was constantly complimenting her. If she were a vain kind of woman, all his praise would've gone to her head by now.

He held the passenger door open for her and once she was settled in the seat, closed it and headed around to the driver's side. He started the car and headed for the road. He drove off the Army post, then glanced at her. "Close your eyes."

"What?"

"Close your eyes," he repeated. "You know this town like the back of your hand, and I want our destination to be a surprise."

"I love you," Holly blurted.

For a second, surprise showed in Dash's eyes. But he recovered quickly. "I love you too."

"I just...whatever you've got planned, thank you. But you know I would've been happy spending a quiet night at home with you. The fort you made last year is one of my best memories of our time together."

Dash reached out and palmed the back of her neck gently. His thumb caressed her skin sensually. "Mine too," he agreed. "And you're welcome. Now, stop stalling and close your eyes."

Holly chuckled. She grabbed his hand, kissed the palm, and closed her eyes.

Dash twined his fingers with hers and rested their connected hands on the console between them.

Within a minute or so, Holly was completely lost. She'd tried to keep track of where Dash was driving, but he must've taken extra turns on purpose, because she couldn't envision where he was taking her.

Ten minutes later, he stopped the car. "Stay here with your eyes shut," he ordered. "I'm coming around to get you."

Holly nodded. She heard the driver's side door shut, and she couldn't help but feel a bolt of excitement go through her. Dash loved her. He was attentive and generous. But he wasn't the most romantic man in the world. Then again, who needed grand gestures when they had a man who did household chores without having to be nagged, who gladly dragged the trash can to the curb once a week, who put up with her love of rom-com movies, picked up a romance book he saw at the grocery store just because he thought she might like it, and who never complained about having to sleep in the wet spot after they made love?

Thinking about how that wet spot always came to be made Holly smile. On top of all his other good qualities was the fact that Dash was an amazing lover. He always made sure she had an orgasm, or two, when they made love. She'd never imagined this would be her life, and she'd do whatever it took to keep it.

Holly jumped when the door next to her opened. Dash chuckled.

"Did you forget I was here?" he asked.

"No," Holly lied, not wanting to admit she'd been lost in her head.

He laughed once more and tingles went down Holly's spine. She was glad he didn't call her on her daydreaming. He touched her arm, then took her hand in his. "Leave the flowers here, we'll get them later. Come on, up you go," he said.

Holly stood up and didn't feel at all apprehensive about walking with her eyes closed. She knew without a shadow of a doubt that Dash would never let her fall or get hurt. He wrapped his arm around her waist and she leaned against him as they walked.

Without a word, he steered them forward. The ground they were walking on changed from concrete or asphalt to grass. She could hear birds chirping overhead and the sound of cars driving nearby.

Dash stopped them and turned her. His hands rested on her shoulders for a moment before he said, "You can open your eyes now."

Holly blinked a few times, trying to let her eyes adjust to the light once more.

The first thing she saw was Dash's beautiful hazel eyes. He had long lashes that ought to be illegal on a man. He was staring down at her with so much love, she immediately felt her throat closing up with emotion.

"I love you, Holly Culver," he said in a low, earnest tone. "You're the shining light in my life. Everything I do has more meaning now that I have you. I feel as if I was just going through the motions of living before I met you. You make me want to be a better person simply so you'll be proud of me."

"I *am* proud of you," Holly couldn't help but interrupt. She hadn't looked around to see where he'd brought her, being content to just stare at her man. He was so damn handsome in his uniform.

Dash leaned down and kissed her forehead tenderly. Then he physically turned her so she was standing with her back to him.

Holly gasped at the sight in front of her.

She immediately recognized it as Dash's small backyard, but it had been totally transformed. A large white tent had been erected, complete with white fairy lights. A lone table sat under it with a white tablecloth and two place settings. Two huge bouquets of flowers on pedestals were arranged near the table, along with a bottle of what she figured was probably champagne chilling in an elevated bucket. Off to the left of the yard were a big screen and a projector, along with a loveseat, and a ton of blankets and pillows.

It was the most romantic thing Holly had ever seen. She turned to tell Dash that it was all too much

—and was surprised to see her man on one knee. He was smiling up at her...with a small black box in his hand.

Tears immediately sprang to Holly's eyes. "What? How? Dash..."

"I've been thinking about doing this for close to a year," Dash said. "I've loved you from almost the first time I saw you. I know a lot of people dismiss love at first sight, but I know for a fact it's a real thing. I love you, Holly. Will you marry me? I know being with a Delta Force soldier isn't easy, but you've proven over the last year that you can handle it. Can handle *me*. Please make me the happiest man in the world and say you'll be mine forever."

"Yes," Holly managed to say even though she was crying. "Although you should know that I'll be yours forever even if we aren't married. Just as you're mine."

Dash smiled and stood up. He took her hand in his and slipped a ring with a huge pear-shaped diamond down her finger.

"Oh my gosh, Dash! It's huge!"

"That's what she said," he teased.

Holly burst out laughing. She threw herself at her fiancé and knew she was smiling like a loon. "I love you so much!" she exclaimed.

When Dash put her on her feet again, she gestured toward the yard. "This is amazing."

"Yup. Come on, dinner's probably ready to be served."

"Served? Jeez, Dash, did you hire waiters?"

"Yup," he said without hesitation. "And a chef too. I know how you feel about fancy restaurants, so I decided to bring the restaurant to you. Here. Where you can feel comfortable and you don't have to put on dress-up clothes. And I've got *The Truth about Cats and Dogs* all cued up for us to watch after we eat."

"I love that movie," Holly whispered.

"I know," Dash said with a tender smile.

Holly cozied up to her man and put her arms around his shoulders. "This is the best Valentine's Day ever," she whispered.

"So far," Dash corrected.

"You can't top this. Ever," Holly said firmly. She recognized the stubborn look on her man's face. "That wasn't a challenge," she added.

"Uh-huh," he said.

Damn, she loved this man. "I've heard that an engagement isn't final until it's sealed with a kiss."

"Is that so?" Dash asked.

"Yup."

"Well, in that case, I'd better make this super-duper official so no one tries to say I didn't follow all the rules."

He lowered his head, and Holly went up on her

tiptoes to meet him halfway. The kiss was long, deep, and felt different from any kiss they'd ever shared before. By the time Dash lifted his head, Holly was ready to tear his uniform off and have her wicked way with him right there, not caring who might walk out and see them.

"Hold that thought," Dash said gruffly.

His erection pressed against her belly and it was obvious he was just as turned on as Holly was. "You gonna be able to walk like that?" she teased, pressing her hips into his groin playfully.

"I've gotten really good at figuring it out since I'm this way all the time around you," Dash told her. "Come on, let's eat. Then we can change into more comfortable clothes, and come back out here when it's dark and snuggle under the blankets and watch your movie. I've got some portable heaters I can set up after the sun goes down so we don't get too cold. And just so you know, there's a flap we can close so we'll have complete privacy out here."

"Sex in our backyard fort? I'm so down for that," Holly said with a grin.

"I figured you might be," Dash answered with a chuckle.

———

Hours later, after a delicious meal of steak and lobster; after they drank the entire bottle of champagne; after Holly had texted a picture of her ring to Stella, and gotten a return picture of Stella's own ring that Magic gave her when he proposed; after they'd changed into more comfortable clothes and watched the movie; and after Dash had shown her without words how much she meant to him, Holly lay naked and replete in his arms on the love seat.

She was cozy and warm thanks to Dash's body heat and the propane heaters he'd set up. She was snuggled up against his side, tracing circles on his chest as she listened to his heartbeat under her cheek.

"Dash?"

"Yeah?"

Holly didn't know why she was whispering, but the moment just seemed to call for it. "I don't think I want a big wedding. Your mom and sisters, my parents and brother, Stella, a few people from work, your Delta team...and that's it. I don't need a huge party, and I don't want to wait months and months to marry you either."

For some reason, she felt Dash's muscles relax under her. She hadn't realized he'd been tense until that moment.

"What?" she asked, picking up her head so she

could look into his eyes. The fairy lights above their heads gave her more than enough illumination to see, but they weren't bright enough to sully the romantic mood of the evening.

"I'm happy you think that way," Dash said. "Because I have another surprise for you."

"Another? I think you've done more than enough, Dash. I've never been so spoiled."

"I love spoiling you," Dash said, then turned his head and kissed her.

Holly almost forgot what they were talking about, but eventually, she pulled back and said, "Another surprise?"

He chuckled. "Right. So, I feel the same way about the small ceremony, and I don't want to wait to marry you either. That's why we have an appointment tomorrow to get our marriage license. This tent actually has a two-fold purpose. The second the seventy-two-hour waiting period is up, I've arranged for an officiant to meet us here. Our parents are arriving tomorrow, and your brother and my sisters get here Monday. If you agree, we can be married on Tuesday."

Holly pushed herself upright, not even noticing that the blanket fell off her shoulders and her boobs were practically in Dash's face. "Seriously?"

"Yes."

Holly's mind spun. She couldn't think straight.

"Is that...if it's too fast, we can wait," Dash said, the uncertainty easy to hear in his tone.

"What? No! I just...holy shit. Yes! I can't believe you've already got it all arranged!" Holly exclaimed.

"I love you. And I can't wait to make you mine permanently. I'd do anything for you, Hol, don't you know that?"

"Oh my gosh, what am I going to wear?" she asked, trying not to panic.

"It's all arranged. I stole that bridal magazine you tried to hide from me and noted the pages you dog-eared. There're four dresses upstairs in our room for you to choose from. We can return the ones you don't choose. The flowers have been ordered. The catering's done. And I even took the liberty of talking to your boss about a honeymoon. It can't be too long because of my job, but I think you'll like the mountain retreat in New Mexico I've booked for us. It's actually a retreat for people who suffer from PTSD, but the owners have assured me that our cabin is secluded and we can be completely alone as much as we want."

Holly was speechless. This man, gah!

"Say something," he begged. "Are you upset that I did all this?"

"Upset? No way!" Holly told him. "I'm relieved

that I don't have to plan anything. Are we really going to be able to be married on Tuesday?"

"Yeah," Dash said. Then his hand came up and covered one of her exposed breasts. He tweaked her nipple, and Holly groaned.

Without another word, he leaned forward and fed her nipple into his mouth. He bit down playfully, then sucked. Hard.

Holly's back arched and she moved so she was straddling Dash on the couch. He immediately lifted his hands and palmed both her breasts, which were hanging free.

"I think you deserve a reward for all you've done," Holly said.

"Yeah?"

"Yeah. I haven't given you my Valentine's Day present yet." Holly knew the picture of the two of them she'd had framed didn't come close to all that Dash had done for her tonight, but she also knew he'd love her gift anyway.

"Saying yes was my present," Dash said without hesitation. "You giving yourself to me is my present. *You* are my Valentine's Day gift, my Christmas and birthday presents for the rest of my life. I don't need anything but you."

Goo. Holly was officially a pile of goo.

"I love you," she whispered.

"And I love you," Dash told her. A glint shone in his eyes. "Now, fuck me."

Holly beamed. "With pleasure."

* * *

Continue reading for Stella & Magic's story!

And book 1 in Susan's new series, SEAL Team Hawaii, *Finding Elodie,* is now available!

Also by Susan Stoker

Delta Team Two Series

Shielding Gillian
Shielding Kinley
Shielding Aspen
Shielding Jayme (novella)
Shielding Riley
Shielding Devyn
Shielding Ember (Sep 2021)
Shielding Sierra (Jan 2022)

SEAL Team Hawaii Series

Finding Elodie
Finding Lexie (Aug 2021)
Finding Kenna (Oct 2021)
Finding Monica (TBA)
Finding Carly (TBA)
Finding Ashlyn (TBA)
Finding Jodelle (TBA)

SEAL of Protection Series

Protecting Caroline
Protecting Alabama
Protecting Fiona
Marrying Caroline (novella)

Protecting Summer

Protecting Cheyenne

Protecting Jessyka

Protecting Julie (novella)

Protecting Melody

Protecting the Future

Protecting Kiera (novella)

Protecting Alabama's Kids (novella)

Protecting Dakota

SEAL of Protection: Legacy Series

Securing Caite

Securing Brenae (novella)

Securing Sidney

Securing Piper

Securing Zoey

Securing Avery

Securing Kalee

Securing Jane

Delta Force Heroes Series

Rescuing Rayne

Rescuing Aimee (novella)

Rescuing Emily

Rescuing Harley

Marrying Emily (novella)

Rescuing Kassie

Rescuing Bryn
Rescuing Casey
Rescuing Sadie (novella)
Rescuing Wendy
Rescuing Mary
Rescuing Macie (novella)
Rescuing Annie (Feb 2022)

Badge of Honor: Texas Heroes Series

Justice for Mackenzie
Justice for Mickie
Justice for Corrie
Justice for Laine (novella)
Shelter for Elizabeth
Justice for Boone
Shelter for Adeline
Shelter for Sophie
Justice for Erin
Justice for Milena
Shelter for Blythe
Justice for Hope
Shelter for Quinn
Shelter for Koren
Shelter for Penelope

Ace Security Series

Claiming Grace

Claiming Alexis
Claiming Bailey
Claiming Felicity
Claiming Sarah

Mountain Mercenaries Series

Defending Allye
Defending Chloe
Defending Morgan
Defending Harlow
Defending Everly
Defending Zara
Defending Raven

Silverstone Series

Trusting Skylar
Trusting Taylor
Trusting Molly (July 2021)
Trusting Cassidy (Dec 2021)

Stand Alone

Falling for the Delta
The Guardian Mist
Nature's Rift
A Princess for Cale
A Moment in Time- A Collection of Short Stories
Another Moment in Time- A Collection of Short Stories

Lambert's Lady

Special Operations Fan Fiction

http://www.AcesPress.com

Beyond Reality Series

Outback Hearts

Flaming Hearts

Frozen Hearts

Writing as Annie George:

Stepbrother Virgin (erotic novella)

ABOUT THE AUTHOR

New York Times, USA Today, and *Wall Street Journal* Bestselling Author Susan Stoker has a heart as big as the state of Texas where she lives, but this all American girl has also spent the last fourteen years living in Missouri, California, Colorado, and Indiana. She's married to a retired Army man who now gets to follow *her* around the country.

She debuted her first series in 2014 and quickly followed that up with the SEAL of Protection Series, which solidified her love of writing and creating stories readers can get lost in.

If you enjoyed this book, or any book, please consider leaving a review. It's appreciated by authors more than you'll know.

www.stokeraces.com
susan@stokeraces.com

facebook.com/authorsusanstoker

twitter.com/Susan_Stoker

instagram.com/authorsusanstoker

goodreads.com/SusanStoker

bookbub.com/authors/susan-stoker

amazon.com/author/susanstoker

STELLA & MAGIC

by Riley Edwards

BLURB FOR STELLA & MAGIC

Magic didn't expect the woman of his dreams to literally fall into his arms, but he'll take it. Especially when he's had an eye on said woman—his next-door neighbor, Stella—for quite some time. Their connection is instant, their chemistry hot, their feelings deep. So deep that Magic has big plans for Valentine's Day. Plans that change in a way no one saw coming...

STELLA & MAGIC

CHAPTER 1

Houston, we have a problem.

Stella French was stuck—in a tree. Sure, it was her bright idea to climb it, but now that she was in said tree with her legs wrapped around a branch, knees bloody, shirt torn, she had to admit—at least to herself—it wasn't one of her best ideas.

"Stella," her best friend, Holly, snapped from below.

Perhaps they'd gone about this the wrong way. Holly was the smaller of the two. Maybe she should've been the one to climb the tree, but Holly wouldn't hear of it. She'd wanted to find the building maintenance guy and ask him to let them into Stella's apartment. They should've done that. But that would mean Stella would have to admit she'd locked herself out of her apartment...again.

Climbing a tree and shimmying over to her neighbor's balcony—her hot-as-hell Delta Force operative's balcony—seemed like the better plan. All she had to do was gain access to his balcony, and Stella could climb over the waist-high wall and she'd be on hers. *Voila*. Easy.

What could go wrong?

What if he's home?

Before Stella could get worked up about finally coming face-to-face with the sexy neighbor she'd been crushing on forever, and what the ramifications could be of trespassing on a Delta operative's balcony, Holly said, "We have a problem."

They totally had a problem.

It was harder than Stella had thought. Hanging from a branch was not all that it was cracked up to be. Stella should've given up when Holly had hoisted her, and the first thing that happened was her shirt snagged on the bark. Stella had barely avoided a complete wardrobe malfunction; but without ripping her shirt wide open, she was able to free herself. The second indication the plan was "cockamamie," as Holly called it, was when Stella had slipped and skinned her knees. That was also when Stella refused to admit defeat, and her determination to execute her crazy plan clicked into place.

What's a little indecent exposure to go along with breaking and entering?

"We don't have a problem," Stella lied.

More than halfway to her destination, Stella channeled all the skills she'd gleaned from watching hours of *American Ninja Warrior* and, hand-over-hand, moved along the branch toward her neighbor's balcony.

"I told you to give me back your spare key," Holly complained, and Stella gritted her teeth.

Ugh. As usual, Holly was right. The last time Stella had locked herself out of her apartment, she'd had to borrow the key she'd given her friend, and as usual, Stella had forgotten to give it back. Now it was a beautiful, unseasonably warm January Sunday afternoon in Texas, and there she was locked out of her apartment—and in a tree.

"Fine. You're right," Stella huffed. "And as soon as I get in, I'll give it back."

A deep rumble of laughter came from below, and Stella rolled her eyes and continued across the branch. "Girl, you need a throat lozenge. Seriously, Holly, you sound like a man when you laugh. Do you have a cold? You should try Ricola, the ones with zinc."

"Abort mission," Holly hissed.

"Are you crazy? I'm almost there."

Two decidedly male voices boomed with laughter. Mid-tree-branch-crawl, Stella looked down and caught sight of her wide-eyed friend, then her gaze shifted slightly to the side and...she was going to die. Not a literal death, no, that would be too easy. A very long, agonizing figurative death.

Magic and his equally gorgeous friend were standing next to Holly, staring up at her.

Otherwise known as hot-next-door-neighbor and hot-next-door-neighbor's-friend.

If that wasn't bad enough, they were in uniform.

"Why didn't you tell me?" Stella hissed.

"I *told* you we had a problem."

"A *problem* is me scraping my knees and blood running down my shins, staining my new pair of white Chucks. A *problem* is me tearing open my shirt. They..." Stella paused for dramatic flair because if there was ever a time where drama was needed, it was right then, with the man she'd been perving over since forever standing on the sidewalk watching her hang from a tree branch, "...are not a problem, they're a... I don't know what they are. What's bigger than a problem?"

Stella's friend was no longer paying attention to her. But the most beautiful pair of green eyes stared up at her, and the man who those eyes belonged to was smiling.

"Are you open to suggestions?" Magic asked.

Bad. That was bad. The sound of his voice sent a shiver up Stella's spine, straight up her arms, and even made her fingers tingle. That was a massive *problem* since her grip was slipping.

As if on cue, Stella lost her grip, and suddenly she found herself plummeting to the ground. But instead of hitting the grass and breaking a hip—or something merciful like smacking her head, causing a traumatic brain injury that would mean blissful short-term memory loss—Stella found herself in a pair of strong arms.

"Gotcha," Magic's deep voice rumbled.

Okay, way better than short-term memory loss.

Another shiver. This one did not roll up her spine; it shot between her legs.

"You're bleeding," Magic noted.

Gah. How embarrassing.

"Yeah, that happened when she said she knew how to climb a tree. Obviously, she's not very good at it," Holly helpfully explained.

Apparently, climbing a tree was not the same as riding a bike. And it was one of those activities that were better left in your youth, when you didn't mind bloody knees and torn tank tops.

"Let's get you upstairs and get your knees cleaned up," Magic went on.

Upstairs. Yes, please.

"She's locked out."

Stella lifted her head off Magic's chest and gave her friend a shut-up face. Holly recognized the silent communication and returned her own no-you-shut-up face.

"Come on, Lucy and Ethel, we'll go to my place and get you cleaned up."

"Um. I'm Stella, and she's Holly."

"She's actually brilliant. I know you wouldn't know by her cockamamie idea to trespass on her neighbor's balcony so she could jump to hers, but she knows five languages, and her IQ is only a few numbers shy of genius," Holly supplied. Then added, "But you know what they say about smart people— they lack common sense. And apparently, they don't get classic TV references either."

The man who'd come with Magic was staring at Holly with something that looked a lot like interest— okay, more like blatant, unabashed interest. Holly was staring at him like the heavens had opened up and all of her wildest dreams had come true.

"I'm Dash," the man introduced himself, stepping forward.

"I'm Holly. Holly Culver."

Holly took Dash's outstretched hand, and now

she looked like all of her wildest fantasies had come to life.

Magic dipped his head, and Stella's breath caught as his chin brushed the side of her face.

"I'm Magic."

Yes, yes, he was. Pure magic. That deep voice, those piercing green eyes, with a mop of black out-of-Army-regulation-length hair; the kind that made a woman want to run her fingers through it. Or tug on it when he was getting down to business between her—

"She'll be fine," Magic said, pulling her from her dirty thoughts.

"Huh?"

"Your friend, Holly. Dash'll take care of her."

Stella tore her gaze from Magic and saw Dash walking Holly in the opposite direction—hand-in-hand. According to the bylaws and covenants of the sister-hood, a sister never left a sister's side. Not even when the hot guy she'd been ogling was dragging her off. Holly was her best friend, and in the five years she'd known her, not once had Stella seen her look at a man with such interest.

"If it makes you feel better, I'll text Dash and tell him you want a picture of his license plate."

Before Stella could comment, Holly looked back, gave her wide-happy-eyes, and brought her hand up, mimicking talking on a phone as she mouthed, *call me later*.

Yeah, Holly was just fine and sure as hell didn't need a save. Stella gave her friend a thumbs-up.

"Damn, you're cute." Magic chuckled, and Stella rested her head back on his shoulder.

"Thanks."

His big body shook with humor, and Stella sighed.

A few minutes later, Magic set Stella on her feet in front of his door. It was then it hit her where she was, so when her lips curved up into what she was sure was a goofy smile, she didn't try to hide it.

"Best idea, ever."

Magic's smooth, deep chuckle echoed in the hall. Her eyes drifted closed and she let the moment wash over her.

Oh, yeah, best idea ever.

CHAPTER 2

W<small>ADE</small> "M<small>AGIC</small>" Jacklin couldn't stop smiling as he searched for his first-aid kit. After months of watching his sexy neighbor and trying to find the right time to approach, she'd literally fallen right into his arms.

He couldn't believe his luck when he saw Stella hanging in the tree, her friend standing below her as if the tiny slip of a woman would actually be able to catch Stella if she fell. It was that thought that had pulled his eyes off his neighbor's ass and quickened his step. As it turned out, Magic had arrived just in time.

But before she fell, Stella and her friend had provided some hilarious banter.

Abort mission.

But it had been Stella bitching about ruining her shoes, then getting tongue-tied about him watching that had clinched the deal. He found his in, and he didn't even have to knock on her door asking to borrow a cup of sugar—which was what he'd planned on doing now that his schedule had lightened and his team wasn't up for rotation.

Magic grabbed his kit and made his way back into the living room, finding Stella right where he'd left her sitting on his couch.

"Your setup is opposite of mine," she told him.

"Yeah?"

"Your kitchen's on the left, mine's on the right," she continued.

Magic glanced over Stella's shoulder to the wall behind her. His bedroom was on the other side, meaning if the floorplan was mirrored, he shared a bedroom wall with Stella. In an effort to stop his mind from wandering to her bedroom—or his, and all the filthy things a gentleman who just met a beautiful woman wouldn't think about doing—he looked back to Stella.

Unfortunately, he wasn't a gentleman, and Stella was beyond beautiful. Tall, with long blonde hair, and striking blue eyes that were so damn pretty his mind went there. He couldn't stop himself from wondering what they'd look like when she was overwhelmed with pleasure. Would they turn hazy when he found the places she liked to be touched? Would the color deepen the closer she got to orgasm?

Magic quickly sat on the coffee table in front of her to hide his now throbbing erection.

He cleared his throat and asked, "So, tell me, what was your plan?"

Pink hit Stella's cheeks, and the throbbing turned into an ache.

Sweet Jesus, she was gorgeous.

"Well..." She trailed off, and her full, kissable lips curved up into a smile. "I thought since our balconies are connected, if I could get onto yours, I'd jump over to mine and let myself in."

There were many reasons her plan was faulty, but Magic ignored them in favor of her *letting* herself into her apartment.

"If you know how to pick a lock, why not just open the front door?"

"I don't know how to pick a lock."

"Then how exactly were you going to let yourself in?"

"The slider's not locked."

That was exactly what he was afraid she'd say.

"Babe, that's dangerous as fuck."

Stella tipped her head to the side, and those blue eyes danced with humor. Not seeing a damn thing funny about her leaving her door unlocked, he didn't return her mirth. Actually, now that Stella was sitting in front of him like a dream come true, Magic didn't find any of it comical. Not her hanging from a tree—her knees scraped, her shirt torn—and he especially didn't find the fall amusing. She could've been seriously hurt.

"If it makes you feel better, I lock it at night."

It didn't make him feel better, not even one single bit. But not only wasn't it his place to lecture her about safety, he also had blood to wipe away, scrapes to clean, and a woman to get to know.

"Lift your leg and rest it on mine," Magic instructed.

Stella quickly followed orders and set her calf on his thigh.

Be a gentleman.

Using the damp washcloth he'd brought along with his kit, he dabbed and wiped the blood, revealing the abrasions that marred her smooth skin.

"Good thing I shaved this morning," she mumbled.

Magic lifted his gaze and immediately wished he hadn't. Twinkling blue eyes met his stare, and the ever-growing ache turned painful.

Damn, she's cute.

Magic wracked his brain for something witty to say, but before he could come up with an idea, she continued, "I hope you're not planning on wiping me down with alcohol. That shit stings."

"Don't worry, I'll blow on it."

Her nose scrunched up, and her brows pulled together in what was supposed to be a frown, but it was her lips that caught his attention. Full, pouty, puckered lips he'd been fantasizing about kissing.

"Defeats the purpose of using alcohol if you blow on it."

"It does?"

And...another head tilt. Christ, this woman was killing him.

"I know you're teasing me, but just to confirm, there are many ways I wouldn't mind swapping spit with you," Stella said. "However, you blowing your germs into an open cut isn't one of them. I quite like my legs and wouldn't want to lose one after it has to be amputated once infection set in from your boy-spit contaminating my battle wound."

Magic couldn't stop the groan slipping from his throat at the thought of swapping spit with Stella.

"Battle wound?" He chuckled.

Her beautiful smile made an appearance, and Magic was mesmerized. Months ago, when he moved into the building, it was one of the first things he'd noticed about his neighbor. Straight up, Stella was gorgeous. She was tall, maybe five-eight or five-nine, so there was no missing her long legs. Great hair, stunning eyes, fantastic tits, but it was her smile that had drawn him in. Any time he saw her, she was smiling—not a fake grin most people gave to strangers—open, genuine, and blinding.

"With that said, I'm curious to know—do you blow on your buddies' boo-boos when you're in the field?"

"My buddies?"

"Your team," she explained. "Do you clean them up and blow on them?"

"I absolutely don't blow on any of them," Magic started. Then asked, "My team?"

"Right. I forget quiet professionals." The saucy wink she added made Magic's dick twitch in his pants. "We're not supposed to talk about it. Like *Fight Club*. First rule about Delta Force is you don't talk about Delta Force."

Stella was being playful, cute, but he couldn't stop the knot from forming in his gut. He hoped he was wrong, but it wouldn't be the first time a woman wanted in his bed just to brag about bagging an operator. Something that in the past never bothered him. But Stella was different, and he was honest enough with himself to admit it would hurt if that's what she wanted—bragging rights.

"Hey. What's wrong? I'm just joking with you. I have clearance, and I've sat through a million OPSEC briefings. I know better than to run my mouth. Not only would I lose my job but I'd never put you or any of the teams at risk."

Magic's body started to relax when he asked, "Your job?"

"I'm a linguist."

"Civilian or military?"

He'd never seen her leave her apartment in uniform but he still needed to ask.

Please say civilian.

"Civilian contractor."

Thank fuck.

"Holly and I both," she went on. "We actually translated the intel for your last mission. One of the other linguists missed something, not because they lacked skill but Holly's been speaking Arabic since she was like ten. She speaks it conversationally so sometimes she picks up on certain things that are easy to miss."

It was easy to hear the pride in Stella's voice when she spoke of her friend. Magic liked that. Too often, people were competitive about the wrong things. There was nothing wrong with wanting to be the best. Hell, it was his job to be the best. But he did that as a team, and it sounded like Stella understood.

"That intel gave us what we needed to bring down some very bad men," Magic said, busying himself with cleaning her leg. "We appreciate what you do."

"Please." She waved off his compliment. "All we do is translate emails and phone calls. You guys do the heavy lifting."

"Lots of moving parts, Stella. We can't do our job if you don't provide us with what we need. We can't get where we're going if others don't do theirs." Magic smoothed the bandage over the worst of the scrapes and tapped her shin. "Other one."

"Wow. You didn't even have to blow."

Christ, she was killing him, and she knew it.

"Other leg."

Stella did as asked, and once she was settled, he set about getting to know her.

"So, five languages?"

"My grandmother is from the Netherlands. She insisted everyone in the family speak Dutch. And since *Oma* refused to speak English in the house, I learned Dutch and English at the same time. She also taught me German. From there, French and Italian were easy to pick up. I found that I loved languages, the different nuances between conversational, written, proper. I know it makes me sound strange, but there it is. I'm a total dork."

"Dutch, German, French, Italian, and Arabic. Impressive."

"And Pashto," Stella added.

"So you know seven languages, including English."

"Well, Holly doesn't count English and Dutch as foreign since she considers those my native tongues."

Magic's hands faltered and he swallowed a groan.

Gentleman, he reminded himself.

But now that he was thinking about her tongue, he couldn't stop his body from responding.

"You're too easy." Stella giggled, and his hands went from clinical to roaming.

"Is that so?" he asked, skimming his fingertips up and around so they could graze the back of her knee.

Magic kept his touch light and used an ungodly amount of control not to go any higher. He was already pressing his luck and had passed gentlemanly, going straight to overly familiar.

"It would seem you are as well," he teased.

"Did you just call me easy?" Her eyes narrowed, but the smile belied the censure.

"Easy? Never. Responsive, yes."

"Responsive, huh?"

Jesus fuck, that smile. It did insane things to him.

"I'm gonna kiss you," Magic warned and watched Stella's smile turned into a sexy smirk.

"Is that so?"

Her eyes flashed—smokey blue crowded with lust. A wave of excitement washed over Magic

Thank fuck.

"Yep. On Tuesday night," he confirmed.

"That's rather specific," she returned.

As much as Magic was enjoying the banter, especially the unhidden disappointment he heard in her voice that he wasn't going to kiss her until Tuesday, he needed to get her on her way or he wouldn't be waiting. And they'd be doing more than kissing.

"I'd like to tell you I'm a gentleman, but that would be a lie. And since I don't lie, I figure the best I can do is wait until after our second date. But so we're clear, it's gonna be painful, it might drive me over the edge, it's gonna take all of my control to go slow. So, Tuesday."

"It's Sunday."

"Yep," he unnecessarily confirmed.

"And Tuesday will be our second date?"

"Yep."

"Cocky much?"

"Cocky? No. Confident, determined? Hell yeah. When I see something I want, I don't dally getting it."

"Dally?" She giggled, and Magic took a moment to enjoy the sound.

"No games, Stella. I want to take you out tomorrow. Then Tuesday, I wanna see you again. Not because I wanna kiss you—which, babe, you gotta know I seriously wanna kiss you—but because I've been waiting months to find the right time to ask you out. And since we've been sitting here...no, since I saw you hanging from that tree mumbling under your breath to your girl, I'm kicking my own ass for not finding the time sooner. Straight up, I wanted to ask you out because you've got a great smile. But now I know with those legs, that shiny blonde hair, those beautiful eyes, comes a great personality and good sense of humor." Magic paused to fully appreciate the woman in front of him. The teasing lust had drained away and softness had crept in. Oh, hell, yeah, he wanted more of her. "Not only am I kicking my own ass, I'm pissed I've lost months with you. So no, I'm not gonna dally."

"No games, Magic," she mimicked. "I've been watching you for months, hoping I'd accidentally bump into you and could find a way to charm you into asking me out. If I'd known all I had to do was lock myself out of my apartment and climb a tree, I would've done it months ago." Stella stopped and gave him one of her trademark smiles. "What time should I be ready?"

"Seven."

"I'll be ready at six forty-five."

There it was. No games.

Now all he had to do was find it in him to wait until Tuesday before he kissed her.

CHAPTER 3

A WEEK LATER, there was a knock on the door—not the front door, the slider that led to the balcony. Stella craned her neck and watched Magic walk into her apartment.

"Hey," she greeted and turned back to the stove.

It took several seconds for him to return her welcome, but when he did, his was way better.

Way better.

With his chest fitted against Stella's back, he brushed the hair away from her neck, and a shiver went through her when she felt his lips brush the sensitive skin under her ear.

"Good day?" he asked, not straightening. She felt his lips move against her, which caused another tremble.

He was good at this—the foreplay. So good, it was a miracle she'd held out as long as she had.

Tonight was date number six. Date number one ended with him walking her to her front door. With his hands shoved into his pockets, as he waited for her to enter. The effort it took for him not to touch her wasn't lost on Stella.

Date number two ended with Magic coming into her apartment, closing the door, then he proceeded to rock her world. The kiss he'd warned her about wasn't a kiss, not in the traditional sense. Their lips had indeed met, their tongues had tangled, but it was *more*. Unlike any kiss she'd ever received.

Magic didn't coax—he took, he tasted, he owned. He'd fisted her hair and held her steady while his other hand, resting on her hip, hadn't roamed. His mouth had done all the work, and by the time he broke the kiss, Stella was wet, needy, and panting. More turned-on than she'd ever been in her whole life.

That was, until the end of dates three through five, which had happened consecutively. Each night had ended with a mind-bending, toe-curling kiss, but Magic hadn't taken it any further.

She'd had dinner at his house, he'd eaten at hers, they'd watched movies, laughed themselves stupid swapping stories. They'd talked about all their favorites, what they disliked, places they'd been. Stella knew he had two brothers and a sister. He knew she was an only child. Both their parents were still married. Big stuff, little stuff, deep conversations, silly, flirty banter. In six days, they'd done it all.

Therefore, Stella knew she wanted more—as in everything. Six days was all it took for him to weave his magic, and while she knew his ability to make a woman fall in love with him by date two was not how he got his nickname, it should've been. What had started out as a crush on her sexy neighbor had turned into adoration for a good man.

"Babe?" he called when she didn't answer.

"I want you to spend the night," she blurted out.

She felt his body go solid behind her and she instantly regretted her request.

"Stella," he groaned, and she beat back the quiver. "I'm trying."

When he said no more, she asked, "Trying to what? Drive me crazy? Make me buy stock in Tide or Proctor & Gamble since I do more laundry now—"

"Laundry?"

"Panties, Magic. You can't just leave them in the hamper when they're..."

"When they're what, Stella, pray tell how you can't leave your panties?"

Oh, well, in for a penny, in for a pound.

"Wet. I can't just toss them in with my other clothes soaking wet. They require a handwash after you leave."

That big body of his was shaking and she knew he was laughing at her, something he did a lot, something she loved to watch him do. On more than one occasion, she'd told him an embarrassing story just to see the laugh lines around his eyes appear. But right then, she was enjoying *feeling* his chuckle.

"I had no idea," he said through his mirth.

"You don't leave a wet towel in the hamper, do you? It'll mildew."

Suddenly Magic wasn't chuckling. He was roaring with it, taking her right along with him. Then realization set in and mortification crept up fast and swift. Oh, God, she'd compared her panties to a wet towel. Mildewed panties...gross.

"Smart thinking, washing them out."

"Ugh!"

The shaking stopped and Magic dropped a kiss on her neck and she lost the battle. Full. Body. Quake.

What could she say? His lips did crazy things to her, hence the wet panties and building the courage to ask him to spend the night. Obviously, he knew "spend the night" was code for "let's get naked and busy."

"No games," he said, and she nodded her agreement even though it wasn't a question. "Every night, starting from the first time you were sitting on my couch, it's been torture leaving you. But the last four since I've kissed you have been hell. And by that, I mean extremely painful but necessary."

Stella turned in his arms and pushed him back so they were away from the stove and Magic was leaning on the opposite counter.

"Why have you walked away?"

The question had been burning in her brain. Had she read the signals wrong? She didn't think so. It wasn't like she hadn't felt his erection pressed against her while he kissed her. She could feel him straining not to touch her and take them any further than kissing. So why was he pumping the breaks when she desperately wanted him to pump *into* something else?

"This is different. *You're* different."

"Different how?"

The longer he took her in, the more nervous she became.

"Infinitely different." Magic stopped speaking and her heart stopped right along with his words.

Please be falling in love with me. Please be falling in love with me. Please be falling in love with me. Stella silently chanted, waiting for Magic to continue. *Please. Please. Please feel the same way I do.*

"I'm falling in love with you," he whispered, and

she would've sunk to the floor in relief if he hadn't been holding on to her.

"Thank God." The two words puffed from her mouth, sounding as breathless as she was.

"I take it you feel the same?" He beamed.

God, he had a great smile. Or was he smirking? Yeah, it looked a little cocky, a little roguish, and a whole lot sexy.

Never mind relief, if he kept grinning at her like that they'd be on the floor for a different reason. Oh, there'd be relief—but the sexual-gratification kind that came from fantastic orgasms.

"No games. I fell in love with you when you told me about playing soccer with the kids in Columbia."

"That was our first date," he said, no longer smiling.

"No, that's not right. I fell in love with you when you caught me when I fell out of the tree."

"That was pretty good, wasn't it? Straight-up romance novel shit right there."

Stella narrowed her eyes and shook her head. "Romance novels aren't shit, Magic. You should read one. You might learn a thing or two."

"Are you saying I suck at wooing?" Stella couldn't stop the burst of laughter at her big, strong, tough Delta Operator. "Come on, you have to admit, I give good woo."

"You give good something, and I'm hoping tonight you'll give me more."

"More?"

"A lot more."

Magic's lips curved up and his eyes danced. It was a good look, though in the time she'd spent with him —even during the serious moments—she'd hadn't found a time when he didn't look ridiculously handsome. With Magic, there were varying degrees of sexy —some understated, some outrageously hot. She was surprised she'd managed not to strip him naked.

Stella lost sight of his smile when he dipped his head. The moment of disappointment was erased when his lips met hers.

And once again, with a kiss, he rocked her world. No, he wrought devastation; the best kind where you knew that your life would be forever altered, changed in a way where you knew nothing would ever be as good, pain that was so pleasurable it was like a drug. A habit you never wanted to kick because it fed your soul, made you so happy you wanted to dance and sing and shout.

Unlike all the other times he'd kissed her, he started with soft, teasing flicks of his tongue. He licked her bottom lip and enticed her to do the same. Needing to get closer, Stella rolled up on her toes and pressed tight. Then she engaged her hands. One went under his tee and she moaned when his stomach muscles contracted under her palm.

God Bless America.

Not to be left behind, Magic's hands got with the program. One cupped her breast—unfortunately not under her shirt—and the other grabbed her bottom and he hauled her closer. His erection pressed long and hard against her—so close but too far away—his mouth on hers, his hands finally touching, there was nothing for Stella to do but groan.

"Christ," he snarled when he broke away. Stella's vision was still hazy when he pressed a chaste kiss to the corner of her mouth and whispered, "You're a dream come true."

Oh. My. God.

Her breath caught, her lungs burned, and wetness hit her eyes. There was something Stella needed to say but she couldn't. The words were buried under a mountain of emotions.

"I'm thirty-six," she said. "I've never...no one's ever...I haven't..." She knew she was rambling but couldn't form a coherent thought.

Unable to keep her head up any longer, Stella dropped it to Magic's shoulder and continued to blather.

"I didn't believe it was real. Not the insta-love stuff, not the love at first sight, not the butterflies in your belly. But mostly, I didn't believe *I* could ever feel something this big. So, now, no games, I love you, Magic. So damn much it scares the pants off me, and not in a down-and-dirty fun way but in a way that I know I'll never feel this way again, not with anyone else. And it only took you six days to make me feel it. I'm scared that in another six, I'll be in so deep I'll be drowning."

The more she spoke, the tighter his arms squeezed, which meant the next thing he said made her smile.

"We'll drown together."

She already was.

"And don't be scared, I'm right there with you. Every step. Me and you."

"Every step." Stella turned her head and burrowed under his chin. "Me and you."

"Me and you," he confirmed.

And just like that, she was no longer scared. How could she be—she was surrounded by Magic.

***

Stella was standing at the sink tapping out the last of her text message to Holly when she heard Magic chuckle from behind her. Then she felt her hair slide off her shoulder and she knew what that meant.

Moments later, his lips brushed under her ear and she shivered.

Every time.

By her count, Magic had an accuracy rate of a hundred percent. Once he'd found the secret spot that made her tremble, he hit his target with shocking precision.

"So you're planning on sleeping in tomorrow?" he asked.

Stella glanced over the text string and her cheeks heated.

Stella: You nervous about tonight?

Holly: A little. It's the first time I'll be hanging out with Dash at his place. Are you nervous?

Stella: Hell no! I've been ready for some Magic in my life since he first moved next door!

Holly: Maybe down the line we could double date or something.

Stella: Oh, that's definitely happening! Have fun! Don't do anything I wouldn't do.

Holly: Which leaves me open to just about anything.

Stella: Lol. You know it. Text or call me tomorrow...but not too early. I'm fully expecting to sleep in *wink wink*

Holly: Love you

Stella: Love you too, girl!

The "love you, too, girl" was the last text she'd sent, and knowing she wouldn't hear from Holly again, seeing as she would be with Dash for the rest of the night, Stella exited out of the messaging app and tossed her phone on the counter.

"You know it's rude to read over someone's shoulder, right?"

"Just gathering intel." He smiled, and since his mouth was still on her neck, she not only heard him but felt the words dance over her skin.

Something he knew she loved because she'd told him.

"Are you breathing on my neck to muddle my mind so I won't be irritated you've read my texts?"

"Is it working?"

"Yeah."

"You need some Magic in your life, Stella?"

"Oh, yeah."

He wrapped his arm around her middle, buried his face in her neck, and busted out laughing.

***

"Good dinner, babe," Magic said on his approach to the couch.

"Thanks for doing the dishes."

"You cook. I clean."

"Is that part of the wooing? Washing dishes? Because if it is, it's totally working."

Instead of sitting next to her Magic tagged her hand and pulled her to her feet.

"What—" The rest of her question was cut short and she squealed as he swung her up into his arms.

"Time for bed."

Stella's arms went around his neck, her belly flip-flopped, and she took in a stuttering breath to calm her excitement. By the time Magic made it to her room, she was ready to tear her clothes off and he hadn't done anything but carry her.

Once she was back on her feet, she wasted no time grabbing the hem of Magic's tee and pulling it up. Thankfully, he took pity on her and yanked it off the rest of the way.

"Holy smokes," she mumbled, taking a step back so she could fully appreciate the beauty in front of her.

And that's what it was, pure male beauty. There was no other way to describe Magic. Smooth skin, perfect ridges and valleys made up his washboard abs, but it was his chest and shoulders that held her attention. She knew he was strong, had seen the sleeves of his t-shirts pulled tight against his biceps, had felt some of the hardness under her hands, but she hadn't known the goodness that awaited under the fabric.

Hers. It was all hers.

"Come here."

"Nope. I'm not done staring at you."

"How about you come here and I'll give you more to look at?"

Stella's gaze snapped to his, and he smiled.

"What's wrong? No witty comeback?"

She would've had one if her lust-addled brain had been working, but seeing the man shirtless had her dumbstruck.

It was a good thing Magic didn't seem to have the same problem. He took the two steps needed, hooked her around her waist, dipped in, and laid a long, wet, deep kiss on her, and that was all it took for all stations to get back online. After that it was a frenzy—hands tugged at fabric, her t-shirt was off and sailing through the air, bra and panties discarded, cargo pants and boxers a heap on the floor.

And through all that, skin was explored, tongues clashed, hair was pulled, and hunger built.

"Bed," he rumbled and desire shot straight to her center.

Stella uncurled her fingers from around his neck and scrambled back until she felt the mattress hit the back of her knees, and in an uncoordinated, unladylike manner, she got on the bed. They'd never played games, they'd never hidden their attraction. Magic had told her many times he thought she was sexy and beautiful, and she believed him. All of that meant she was not shy when she lay back completely bared to him.

Apparently, he felt the same way, standing in front of her comfortable in his nudity, as he should be. His body was a work of art, cut from granite, hard everywhere.

Every. Where.

Strong thighs. Muscles stacked on top of muscles —all of that hot—but right then, Stella was fixated on something else. Oh, yeah, he was hard and strong and thick. And when his hand came up and fisted his dick, she didn't miss it. Neither did she miss the way his hand stroked—tight grip, long, slow glides. The erotic sight in front of her was the hottest thing she'd ever witnessed. A sight she'd gladly watch for hours, but the pulsing between her legs couldn't be ignored.

Her eyes sliced to Magic's and she felt it, everything he was trying to convey with a look. His need, his hunger, his love, his excitement—she felt it all. It coursed through her veins and set her on fire.

Thankfully, he moved, taking a step closer. But before he made it to the bed he stopped, bent down, and reached for his cargos. Since he was gloriously naked, Stella had a bird's-eye view of those muscles bunching and straining as he unearthed a condom and tossed it on the bed.

"Feeling lucky?" Stella asked, gesturing at the square wrapper at her hip.

"Fuck yeah." His knee went to the bed and her heart rate doubled. "You should know, I am absolutely the lucky one in this bed, but by the time I'm done with you, you're gonna swear it was you."

Stella had no doubt she'd be getting lucky, didn't think for a second she hadn't struck gold when she'd fallen into his arms, but she loved that he thought he was the lucky one to have her.

"I'm gonna swear it, huh?" she teased, and Magic gave her a new kind of smile, one she hadn't seen before—wolfish, predatory, seriously hot.

He picked up her foot and kissed her ankle, then her calf, and higher still until his tongue grazed the inside of her thigh. Tiny pinpricks of heat rose to the surface until she was so hot she squirmed.

"My sweet Stella," he murmured and continued to lick. "You have no idea."

Closer and closer, achingly slow, so slow she fought the urge to yank his head where she needed. So slow she thought she'd die from want. Then he was *so* close, his tongue grazed over her pussy.

"Oh God," she moaned.

"Mmm," Magic hummed, lifting her leg over his shoulder. "Keep 'em nice and wide, baby, so I can eat you."

A long, slow swipe of his tongue had her groaning, "Oh. My. God."

"You taste so damn good." *Swipe.* "So damn good." *Swipe.* "Bet you'll taste even better when you come in my mouth."

"Magic."

"Yeah, baby?"

"Hurry."

The wolfish smile made a reappearance and she hummed—actually hummed—her approval.

"My beautiful, sweet Stella, all laid out for me. Pretty pussy wet." Magic paused and circled her opening with his fingertip, skimming the sensitive flesh, spreading her excitement up to her clit, then back down. "Maybe I wanna watch you come on my fingers first."

Two thick fingers invaded and her back arched. Desire thrummed through her veins. Time stopped. Everything slowed. Then Magic went about proving he was right. She had no clue.

"So beautiful." That was all she heard before he lowered his head and sucked her clit between his lips. On their own accord, her hips worked in time with his plunging fingers. Reaching, searching, almost there.

His teeth scraped her clit and that was all it took. Bright, blinding pleasure consumed her until she was screaming her orgasm.

It was glorious.

Stella bit back another moan when his tongue slowed, gently licking, bringing her down from the earth-shattering climax.

"Still want more?" Magic's chuckle brought her back to the room.

"Oh, yeah."

Boneless and happily wrung out, thankfully she had the foresight to open her eyes in time to see Magic lift to his knees and grab the condom.

Son of a mother trucker.

Long and thick and hard with a pearl of wetness dripping from the tip.

She licked her lips and smiled when Magic groaned. Without taking her eyes off the cock in front of her, she asked, "Do I get a taste?"

"Next round," he said and rolled the latex down his erection.

Well, that was disappointing. Though the blow of denial was short-lived. So short-lived she'd forgotten all about wanting to get him in her mouth when he bent forward and his lips went to her belly. Long trailing kisses slowly moved over her stomach up to her breasts, where he stopped to tongue one nipple, then the other. Magic made his way up to her neck, working her favorite spot until she was squirming and panting.

He dropped a sweet kiss on her lips before he lowered himself over her. Warm and safe—those were her thoughts as Magic hitched one of her legs around his waist, forcing her legs wider, making a place for himself. Then she felt the head of his dick notch into her pussy and a whole slew of new dirty thoughts raced in.

"Magic." The complaint came out as a whine, and if he didn't hurry, she'd beg. She was ready, so, so ready; any second she'd roll him to his back and take over.

"You're gonna want to hold on for this."

"You think so, huh?" she teased.

His answer was nonverbal but effective.

In one hard drive that jolted her body, Magic filled her full.

"Oh, God."

Her arms went around him, her ankles locked, and she held on.

"Now you're ready."

She was so ready. Beyond ready. As a matter of fact, she'd been ready since the day he caught her.

"Magic."

His eyes cut to hers and he started moving. Tender and slow. Long drugging strokes—kindling on a fire. Every in and out stoked the flames until the blaze seared and electricity sparked—the telltale signs of the approaching explosion.

With all four limbs wrapped around him, holding tight, clutching his cock, she detonated. Pleasure tore through her fast and sharp. Everything tingled, from the tips of her fingers to her toes, and throughout the rush of ecstasy, Magic rode her, prolonging the euphoria.

"Still want more?"

Slowly Stella blinked away the haze and stared up at Magic, too lust-drunk to respond.

But he didn't need her to, he went on. "Smokey blue. Every night I dreamed about your eyes. I dreamed about your smile. I dreamed about kissing you. I dreamed about being right here. Every night. Dream come true. All of you."

Damn, he was good at that. So much better at heartfelt words than she was. Snarky comebacks—hell yeah. Hearts and flowers and declarations—not so much.

"I'm never letting go," she lamely returned.

"That's good, seeing as you're mine."

Cocky.

"Now that I have your attention, you ready for more?"

"Oh, yeah."

"Hands on the headboard and brace."

She unwrapped her arms and moved them above her head and asked, "Like this?"

"Arch your back." Magic shifted and his cock slipped deeper. "Fuck, my sweet Stella, so damn sexy."

After that, Magic got down to business and brought home a triple.

***

It was the ringtone that woke Magic. The only reason he was reaching for Stella's phone was because he knew it was Holly. If something was wrong, his woman would want to know. The screen was still lit and the text visible.

Holly: Definitely a 12 on a scale of 1 to 10.

Magic's lips twitched.

A twelve, huh? Good for Dash. Better for Holly.

Seriously fucking good for Magic.

He rolled, taking a naked Stella with him, and decided on a course of action.

"Magic?"

Fuck, he loved her voice. "Wake up, baby."

"Huh? Why?"

"I wanna show you something," he told her and

lowered his mouth to her nipple and drew it into his mouth.

"Show me what?"

His tongue swirled around the now-hard peak and he answered, "What a thirteen looks like."

"A thirteen?"

"A thirteen," he confirmed. Then added, "Hands and knees, baby, I'm gonna show you just how dirty a thirteen is."

"Oh, God."

An hour later when they bedded down, sweaty and spent, Stella mumbled, "That wasn't dirty, that was filthy."

Hell yeah it was. It was also shrouded in love and the best sex he'd ever had.

CHAPTER 4

MAGIC PULLED his cell from his pocket to text Stella and saw he'd missed a text while he was in his brief.

Stella: Change of plans. I'll meet you at the picnic table.

There were smiley faces, hearts, and a green alien after the message.

Pure Stella. Cute.

"You got plans?" Dash asked as he made his way out into the hallway.

"Meeting Stella."

His friend looked like he wanted to give him shit about the amount of time he spent with Stella, even though Dash hadn't missed an opportunity to spend time with Holly either.

Over the last month, he'd taken his woman out to lunch every day. They usually stayed on post since they both only got an hour, but they still connected even though they woke up together every morning. Magic knew it wouldn't last forever, so he was taking advantage. Work-ups would start up again soon, and then there was always the possibility he could get called up for a mission with next to no notice. Which would mean from call-in to wheels-up, he could be flying across the ocean within a few hours. So, yeah, he was taking all he could get, but he was also giving Stella what she needed to get her through the times she wouldn't have him.

Even though she was a civilian, she understood the rigors of his job. Actually, there might be times she'd know before him if he was getting ready to deploy, depending on the intel she translated. She'd told him repeatedly she knew what she was getting into and had no problem with his unpredictable schedule, and he believed her. Stella was the most independent woman he knew. She and Holly had once talked about moving in together but decided they both liked their privacy and alone time. That was something else about Stella that Magic liked, she was totally comfortable in her own company.

"You look like you're in pain," Magic continued.

"And you look like you're asking for a busted lip," Dash volleyed with no heat.

"Just saying, it looks painful, you not cracking a

joke about the time I spend with Stella, knowing I got a whole arsenal of comebacks about how much time you spend with your woman."

A look Magic didn't like stole over his friend's expression. The man looked smug—and knowing Dash the way he did that could mean bad news for Magic.

"How's your ass?" Dash inquired.

"Come again?"

Unable to contain his laughter, Dash lost the battle, and in the hallway outside of the briefing room where the rest of his teammates were still congregated Dash busted a gut. His laughter echoed on the walls, magnifying the sound and drawing unwanted attention.

Stella.

His sweet Stella was an over-sharer.

"Your ass..." Dash sputtered. "I hope you got cream on those burns."

Asshole.

"You don't put cream on rug burns, dipshit."

"Right."

Fucking Dash.

"How's *your* ass? Heard all about the slip and fall in the shower. Dropped the soap, did ya?"

One...two...and there it was.

Recognition dawned and Dash flushed.

"Dude, you're blushing," Magic pointed out.

"I'm confiscating that damn cellphone," Dash grumbled.

"Good luck with that."

With a lift of his chin Magic left his friend still mumbling about text messages. Dash didn't give a shit the women shared. He didn't either. Mostly it was amusing...unless Magic had carpet burns on his ass because his woman had met him at the front door and had been in a certain kind of mood. A mood Magic wholeheartedly agreed with. Mentioning the text message was a joke, a segue into busting his buddy's chops about falling in the shower, and had nothing to do with Stella's enthusiastic greeting. No, that was all about the flowers he'd sent her.

Mental note: order more flowers for Valentine's Day tomorrow.

Magic made his way around the side of Division HQ, staying on the sidewalk, careful not to step on the precious grass that would get him an ass-chewing if he dared cut across it. His thoughts went from the time cutting across the parade grounds would save him to tomorrow night's plans. He wanted everything perfect for his first Valentine's Day with Stella, the woman who had quickly become the center of his universe. She deserved the memory, something special she could tell their children about. It was too soon for a ring. Though if he thought he could get away with it, he'd ask her to marry him and slip a big, fat diamond on her finger.

As it was, he was going to push his luck and ask her to move in with him, or him with her. This two-apartment shit was silly. They lived next door to each other, shared a wall, all they'd done since the first night they'd slept together was bed hop. His or hers —that was the question, not *if* they'd be sleeping together.

The sound of gunfire rent the air, and Magic froze. His hand went to his hip and he cursed when he didn't find his sidearm.

The second burst of gunfire reminded him he was not in the desert, he was on post, meeting Stella for lunch.

Stella.

Fuck.

Without a second thought about the shooter's location, Magic took off in a sprint toward the picnic area. His only objective was to get Stella to safety; then and only then would he look for the gunman. His heartrate spiked when he thought of her sitting on top of the bench waiting for him. His beautiful

Stella would be an easy target. There wasn't even a goddamn tree she could use as cover.

More shots, coupled with panic-filled shouts and high-pitched screaming as he rounded the corner. Not breaking stride, he scanned the area, not seeing the shooter. The parking lot for the post exchange was full as was the lot for the commissary. Too many cars to hide behind, too many damn people running for cover. Total mayhem.

Another volley coupled with glass shattering pushed him to run faster. The daycare center just beyond the picnic area came into view and anger started to tick up his spine. It was the middle of the day, the center would be full of children.

Where the hell was Dash? Was he meeting Holly at the PX for lunch? Magic hadn't asked, instead, he'd given his friend shit. How the hell had his day turned to shit? One minute he'd been planning the perfect Valentine's Day for his woman, the next, Fort Hood was under attack. A post on US soil.

How in the fuck did that happen?

Easy.

No gun, no comms, no team at his back, a knife in his pocket. Shit odds bringing a knife to a gunfight. Luckily, Magic was good with a blade and he didn't mind messy. Getting close would be the issue. He'd get Stella to safety, take out the shooter, then find Dash.

Fuck, where was Stella?

Sirens wailed in the background just as the picnic table came into view. No Stella. He wasn't sure if that was good or bad. He hoped she'd heard the shots and run. The problem was, which way did she run—to cover or toward the crazy asshole shooting?

He didn't have to wait long for his answer—no cover, no safety, out in the open on her knees. And blood.

Jesus fuck.

Magic's long, pounding strides ate up the distance and he skidded to a halt in front of her and accessed the situation. Their lunch lay abandoned on the benches, Stella uninjured on her knees in the grass leaning over a wounded soldier, blood coating her hands. No shooter in sight, they needed to move.

"Stella."

Wild, scared blue eyes lifted to his and anger turned to murderous intent. No sparkling blue, no joy, no humor—all of that gone. Fear rolled off of her in waves.

Calm. She needed him calm and in control. It was easy to slip into his role now that he knew she was unharmed. This was what he did. This was who he was, a deadly operator, a man he'd hoped she'd never see.

"I saw him running this way then he collapsed. He's been shot. I had to come back for him."

Magic looked back down at the soldier who had indeed taken a bullet to the chest, if the red staining the middle of his uniform was any indication he was critical. A bullet that wouldn't have penetrated if the man had been wearing a vest. A goddamn vest the kid shouldn't have to wear walking around Fort Hood.

"We need to move." Magic reached down to lift Stella but she jerked away. "Stella!"

"I'm not leaving him."

"Neither am I. But we need to move, now. Stand up."

"Oh my God," she whimpered.

He didn't have to look, he felt the hair on the back of his neck stand, alerting him to the danger, the sixth sense that had served him well and saved his ass many times overseas. The intuition that had failed to alert him in time to save his woman.

Fuck.

Stella's face bleached and her body went solid. Magic craned his neck and saw a man in Army uniform running their way holding a semi-auto rifle. Shooter or MP? Confusion and anger warred until

Magic heard the unmistakable battle cry then straight up fury took over.

"*Allahu Akbar.*"

He didn't need to speak Arabic to know what that meant. He'd heard the phrase many times over the years, however, he never thought he'd hear it when his woman was leaning over a bleeding soldier trying to stem the flow of blood from a mortal chest wound. He never thought he'd be unarmed, unable to protect himself and those around him while a man yelled God is the greatest.

Magic maneuvered himself in front of Stella and quelled his impulse to charge the man closing in on them. He had no backup, no sniper in position, no one to lay down cover fire. No communication with his team. His body the only thing between Stella and the barrel of a high-powered rifle. Flesh and bone were no match for the .556 round, but at least the bullet would have to go through him before it hit Stella. He would be her shield.

The man was speaking rapid-fire Arabic, waving his gun around but thankfully not pulling the trigger.

"What's he saying?" Magic asked Stella.

"You don't want to know."

Magic gritted his teeth and pulled up all the patience he could muster, which was to say not much.

When he repeated his question, it was cold and harsh.

"What is he saying?"

"He's saying he must kill infidels. He keeps repeating it. For his brothers, he must kill Americans."

The man standing in front of him was wearing a US military uniform—easy enough to get, but Magic could swear he'd seen him before coming out of the DEFAC. The two bars on the man's chest patch said he was a captain.

What the fuck?

Stella's hand wrapped around Magic's calf. He ignored the way her hand shook. Control. He had to stay in control. Once he beat back the homicidal rage, and the need to scoop up his woman and run subsided, he asked, "What'd he say now?"

"That you're his ticket to paradise."

Magic knew he should be trying to talk the man down, negotiate, but to do that, he'd have to go through Stella, and the thought of her conversing with a madman had Magic's gut churning.

There was a movement in his peripheral; someone had peeked around the corner of the PX building then disappeared. Stella's fingers tightened. She'd seen it too but the gunman had not.

"Keep your eyes down." He wished his order had

come out softer, but the gun pointed at his chest had him on edge.

If he died, Stella would be next.

And that wasn't going to happen.

"Tell him I'm unarmed and will go with him."

"What?"

Christ, he hated the wobble in Stella's voice. He seriously hated asking her to communicate with the asshole but he needed to keep the guy talking, not shooting.

"Tell him, Stella. I'll go with him." He waited a moment, which was a moment too long before he continued. "Now. I need you to trust me and tell him I'm unarmed and—"

Magic's request was cut off when Stella started speaking in Arabic. The shooter's eyes narrowed, either in shock that she spoke his language or outrage at Magic's offer. Either way, it was a bad sign.

"He said, he doesn't need you to go anywhere with him, he's going to kill us both right here."

Fuck. Where the hell were the MPs, and why the fuck wasn't he allowed to wear a sidearm on post? The shit wouldn't have been a problem if he'd been armed with more than a goddamn knife.

It was time to weigh his odds. The man was now five feet from Magic. He'd likely take two bullets before he could sink his blade. The shooter didn't look like he was wearing a vest but to be on the safe side, he'd go for the throat. The man's hands shook, he was amped up full of adrenaline, obviously not well-trained, therefore, he likely wouldn't get in a headshot.

Yeah, Magic could work with that.

"Let go of my leg, baby."

Slowly Stella did as he asked, and Magic shuffled in preparation to launch himself forward. Unfortunately, his plan was hindered when two men popped out from the side of the building.

Lightning-quick, Magic changed his course of action and tackled Stella as a spray of bullets was unleashed.

The sound was deafening, yet he still heard Stella's exhale as he landed on top of her and covered every inch of her body as best he could. Long seconds ticked by and the gunshots stopped. Stella was under him, not making a sound, not moving.

He waited longer then lifted his head to see the gunman on the ground, rifle kicked away, the now unneeded MPs running toward the scene.

Magic rolled to the side and Stella's eyes opened.

"Did that just happen?" she whispered.

"Yeah, baby, it did. Roll to your back so I can check you over."

"I'm not hurt. You...you..." she stammered, then

smokey blue eyes turned to ice. "Don't ever do that again, Magic."

He jolted at the cold tone of her voice. "Did I hurt—"

"I'm not hurt, you big idiot. Don't you *ever* step in front of a gun again. Not ever, Magic. He could've killed you. You would've...I would've..."

Pandemonium ensued. MPs, medics, men, and women swarmed the area, but Magic only had eyes for his woman. He remained on the grass and pulled her into his lap. Her weight comforting, her arms around him meant he relaxed. She was scared, freaked out, and was going into shock. But she was breathing.

"He wasn't going to kill me," he lied.

Stella pulled her face out of his neck and stared at him like he was the stupidest man to ever walk the planet. He should've known better than to try to pull a fast one on his smart girl.

"Okay, baby, how about this? I can't promise you I won't ever put myself between you and something that could harm you, because I will. I'll do it every time, Stella. But I will promise I'll always protect you."

"So basically, you're *promising* me you'll step in front of a gun." The unhappy squint made Magic smile.

"Yeah, Stella, that's what I'm promising."

"He's dead, isn't he? The soldier."

The change of topic nearly gave him whiplash, though he was grateful she wasn't arguing with him. But bringing up the dead soldier she'd tried in vain to save wasn't a place he wanted to go with her. Hell, it was something he wished she'd never seen. But she needed to understand there was nothing she could've done to save him.

"Yeah, he's gone. But Stella, a wound like that, there was nothing you could've done. You gave him the best thing you could give."

"What's that?"

"You. He wasn't alone, he had you by his side. Right now, you might think that's not much but give it a few days and you'll see I'm right. He didn't die alone in the grass, he had you at his side, and for a soldier, that means something."

"Magic!"

Stella jumped at the shout and Magic cursed under his breath.

"It's Dash," he told her and wrapped his arms tighter.

His friend rocked to a halt in front of them and stared down, taking in the blood on Stella's hand. When their eyes met, Magic gave a short jerk of his head toward the soldier who was being carefully covered with someone's ACU blouse until his body could be taken away.

Later. He'd process losing a fellow soldier later. Right now he needed to get his woman up and someplace that was not a crime scene.

"Holly?" Magic inquired.

"Unharmed. She's in the PX."

Magic hadn't needed to verbally ask—he knew Holly was safe and sound. If she wasn't, Dash wouldn't have been standing there, but he wanted Stella to know her friend was okay. More silent communication passed between the men. Years of serving together, being in the worst of conditions, near death, always having each other's back meant they didn't need words. They'd talk later, after they got their women settled.

"I'll bring Stella over after we talk to the MPs," he told Dash, knowing his friend was eager to get back to his woman.

"Sounds good."

Dash took off through the crowd, and Magic exhaled. In and out until his breathing evened and his nerves started to wane.

"I'll get you home as soon as I can."

"Thank you," Stella whispered but didn't lift her head.

And for the first time, when he came down from

the rush of adrenaline and danger, he did it shaking in fear.

Too fucking close.

One bullet. That's all it would've taken, and they both would've been gone.

"Love you, sweet Stella."

Her arms tightened, and she returned, "Love you, too."

CHAPTER 5

STELLA SLOWLY CAME AWAKE to the thump of Magic's heart. She took stock of her surroundings. Warm, hard body under her cheek. A strong arm slanted across her back. Legs tangled. The smell of a man—her man.

Magic.

He was alive. They were alive.

He was also awake but hadn't moved. And he called her sweet Stella, but she should be the one who called him sweet Magic. After a very long day, the worst day she'd ever had in her entire life, Magic had brought her home, sat her on her couch, fed her dinner, then tucked her into bed and held her as she trembled.

It was a different kind of tremble, not the sexy, fun kind she normally felt when she was next to her man. It was gory. Memories of a dead man. She'd shook, remembering the sound of gunshots and screams. Through it all, Magic had held her. Strong. Calm. Unwavering in his support. He let her get it all out.

Now it was the next morning after a seriously shitty day. A morning she thought she'd be curled into a ball of fear and anxiety but instead, she felt safe. Grateful. Magic had saved her life and she knew it. If he hadn't come when he had, she'd be dead. If he hadn't tackled her and used his body as a human shield, she'd be dead.

It was early, she'd only had her eyes open for a few minutes but she made the decision not to dwell upon all the ways yesterday could've been worse, all the bad that had happened. Instead, she vowed to be thankful. If she hadn't already known with every fiber of her being that Magic loved her, yesterday would've proved it.

"I know you're awake," she whispered.

His arm around her tightened and he pressed a soft kiss on the top of her head. What he didn't do was speak.

"Are you okay?"

"I know it's Valentine's Day, and I'll make it up to you, but today we're not leaving this bed."

She didn't need him to make anything up to her.

Spending the day in bed with Magic sounded like the perfect Valentine's Day to her. But she sensed something was wrong so she gave him what he needed.

"Sounds good to me."

"And I want you to move in. Or I'll move in here. I wanted to ask you tonight, I had it all planned out, something romantic, special, a day you'd never forget. A day you could tell our kids about so they'd know how much their old man loved their mom. I want you to have that."

Stella was right, something was very wrong, and it sucked because she wanted to bask in the joy of hearing him talk about their future—one that included children. A future she'd wanted since the first day she'd officially met him. She'd been worried it was too soon to feel so deeply for a man she'd been with for a month but when Stella spoke to her mom about it, she'd learned something new about her parents. A secret that still made her smile.

Her parents had two anniversaries. A special one that no one knew about and the one Stella's grandparents knew about. Her parents had snuck away and gotten married after knowing each other for two weeks. *Two weeks.* They told no one and a year later had a big ceremony for their families. After Stella's mom told her the story, she'd finished with, "It's never too soon to love someone."

So, she knew she wanted the children Magic spoke of, she knew she wanted to live with him. Knew she'd marry him that afternoon if he asked. What she didn't know was how she was going to make Magic feel better.

"I have more stuff than you," Stella started. "But your unit has a remodeled bathroom, which is a plus. And your appliances are newer. However, neither of us has a washer and dryer and I'm tired of hauling my laundry down the stairs."

She paused to gather her thoughts but also to enjoy the way his heart was now pounding against her cheek.

"Maybe it would be better if we found a house," she continued. "Something small, close to post. I don't want a big yard I have to take care of when you're deployed but it'd be nice to have a washer and dryer and a place where we can have a grill and some outside furniture."

"I want a big yard. I'll hire a gardener."

"As long as I'm not pushing a mower in the Texas heat, I'm a-okay with a big yard. Maybe we'll get a dog."

Suddenly Magic's body went stiff. Stella started to push up, but her movement was waylaid when he pinned her to his chest.

"One year," he growled.

"One year? I thought you wanted—"

"We're moving as soon as we can find a house. I can wait one year before my ring's on your finger."

Stella wiggled until his arm loosened enough to climb on top of Magic. Her knees cradled his hips as she sat up on his lap.

"A year?" she semi-repeated.

"A year," he confirmed.

"Hm. I don't know, a year sounds painful."

A knowing smile tipped up his lips and he shook his head in amusement. This was her Magic—playful, happy—not forlorn and wary.

They were alive.

Stella pulled her t-shirt off and tossed it aside, loving the way his eyes flared when her breasts came into view.

"Goddamn, you've got great tits."

Her man was good at flowery declarations of love. He was also good at dirty talk.

"A year might drive you over the edge," she teased and rocked herself against his erection. "Might take all of your control."

"Fuck control," he grunted, and she squeaked in surprise when he surged up and hugged her. "Top or bottom?"

"Top."

"Mm," Magic hummed his approval and lowered

his face to her neck. "My favorite." He paused long enough to brush his lips over her favorite spot. "I get to lie back and enjoy you work your Magic."

"Corny," Stella huffed.

"Not sure about corny but I know someone who's horny."

"Ugh. I hate that word."

"I know you do." He chuckled and lowered himself back down to the bed, taking her with him. "Lean up."

Before she could do as he asked, he was already cupping her breast, his thumb strumming over her nipple until it peaked. Anticipation shafted, lust sparked, need built. And when he drew her closer and traced her areola with his tongue, she hissed her encouragement.

"Horny, baby?" he muttered as he moved to her other nipple.

"Lame," she complained as he lavished her other nipple with his tongue.

"Lame, you say? Tell me, sweet Stella, is this lame?" He quit tonguing and started sucking.

It was then, with her hips grinding, with his mouth working her nipple, she realized Magic was the best lover she'd ever had. Bar none, the best, so good there wasn't a word for how good he was at sex. But what made it better than the best was the teasing banter. He could take her from rolling her eyes at his silly comments to soaking wet and panting in two seconds flat. It was fun, it was exciting, it was great sex, friendship, and love all rolled together.

There were times he made love to her. He could be amazingly tender. Other times he could be dirty and rough and fuck her until she was boneless. Both were equally good. Both left her feeling loved and cherished and safe.

And right then, she felt like fucking. She wanted the heart-pounding, breathless feeling of being alive. She craved the mix of sensations, the softness his eyes would hold but the harsh meeting of their bodies. Top or bottom, it didn't matter; contrary to what Magic, said he never lay back and enjoyed— well, he enjoyed—but he fully participated. He controlled, he took, he gave, and however that came about, it always ended the same way. A screaming orgasm.

"Quit fucking around, baby, or you'll find yourself pinned to the bed."

Stella took a moment to deliberate the merits of being pinned to the bed. There were a variety of pluses to Magic being on top, but since she was in the mood to watch him, she quit fucking around and reached between them. But she took her time and stroked his hard-on over his boxers until he was pumping into her hand.

"Stella," he warned.

Sweet baby Jesus, she loved the way he sounded when he was edgy and hungry. She pulled down his boxers just far enough to unleash his cock and wrapped her fist around his shaft. He groaned his appreciation and when he flexed his hips, she groaned. Hard and thick and all hers.

So what was she waiting for?

As if on cue, Magic reached between them, tore her panties to the side and, with his hand over hers, guided the head of his dick to her center. Then his hand moved to her hip and he slammed her down.

"Fuck," he growled.

Oh, yeah, that was what she'd been waiting for.

Magic losing control was a beautiful thing. If she had the patience to push him there, he turned into a snarly caveman. The results of which were spectacular.

"Good goddamn," he groaned. "Now, Stella, ride me."

Fuel to her flame. Rumbly and full of grit, his voice washed over her and she rocked her hips. And like all the other times before, Magic didn't make her do all the work. His hips thrust up as she ground down, one hand cupped her ass, the other tangled in her hair, his mouth licked, and sucked, and nibbled. Hard and soft, she had the best of both.

But she got better when he pulled off of her nipple and the bossy beast made his appearance.

"Faster, Stella." She went faster. "Jesus fuck. So fucking tight I have to fight coming as soon as I get my cock in you."

"Yes."

Her orgasm danced just out of reach, so close, almost there, as heat tingled up her spine. Goose bumps raced down her back. The explosion so close she could taste it.

"Give it," he demanded and pleasure so painful unfurled and suddenly she couldn't move.

Magic knifed up and, in a smooth, superhuman move, rolled them over, never missing a thrust. Her legs automatically went around his hips, her arms wrapped around his shoulders, and she held on. Unable to hold back, her pussy convulsed and her clit pulsed.

"I. Love. You." Her words were broken and stuttered as she was rocked on all fronts. Mind. Body. Soul. All three alight, all three perfectly aligned.

Magic drove his cock to the root and groaned his release. Every muscle coiled tight, he didn't move.

The moment narrowed. Magic and Stella. All she could see was his face. But she could feel everything.

"I love you, too, my sweet Stella." His words were not broken and stuttered. They were sure and strong. Her legs tightened and his cock twitched and jerked. He didn't grunt or moan through his orgasm. He held her gaze, and since their eyes were locked, she was gifted with the most beautiful sight. Magic undone, bared to her, open and giving everything.

***

"You bake a mean frozen pizza," Stella told Magic as she placed her now-empty plate on her nightstand.

"If you think that was good, wait until you see what I can do with Hot Pockets and a microwave."

"You know, if that's your way of getting out of cooking, you're out of luck. I know you can do more than microwave."

"Right." He winked and pulled her onto his lap. "I forgot I gave you all of my good moves when I was wooing you."

"You're not done wooing, are you?"

"Never."

She believed that—Magic would never be done wooing and she'd never be done working to make him laugh.

No games.

They spent their day in bed. They'd cuddled, they'd talked, they'd snoozed. She'd texted Holly to check on her and learned she and Dash decided to stay in as well. Considering Holly's text had included a weird eggplant emoji, she didn't think her friend was all that torn up about a day alone with her boyfriend. And as far as Stella was concerned, it was the best Valentine's Day she'd ever had. Complete with sex, more sex, frozen pizza, and a bottle of wine.

She didn't know what Magic had originally planned, and she hadn't asked if this was how they'd spend every fourteenth of February. If it was, that would be just fine with her.

"So," she started. "I thought your briefing room would be more..."

"More what?"

She thought about how to explain her reaction to seeing where Magic worked the day before. Frankly, it was a boring room in a boring building. She and Holly had exchanged glances when Magic and Dash escorted the women to the briefing room yesterday, after they'd talked to the MPs. Holly had thought the same thing. Totally boring.

The commander who was in charge of Magic's Delta team had questions about what the captain had said while he was plowing down innocent men and women. The commander had confirmed there had been three fatalities and fourteen had been injured, but none of the injuries were life-threatening. Stella wasn't going to dwell on the bad. Instead, she was going to think about the two soldiers who had tackled the shooter—two brave young men with hearts full of goodness. They'd likely receive medals for their heroic actions—not that that was why they'd leapt into action and saved lives, but they deserved them nonetheless.

"I don't know, I thought it'd be...cooler." She shrugged and went on. "I mean, top-secret missions are planned there. I thought there'd be super-spy gadgets and monitors on the walls with the world's supervillain HVTs on the screens. Or guns and rocket launchers hanging on the wall."

"We put away the super-spy gadgets and rocket launchers when civilians are present." He chuckled.

Stella silently nuzzled closer, enjoying the feel of being close. Just sitting in bed with the man she loved. A lazy day full of nothing important, which made it the specialist of occasions.

"My job's pretty boring."

He was totally lying. Not the bad kind of lie—the little white kind. It was in an effort to downplay what he did. She knew because he did it all the time. He couldn't tell her a lot about his missions; even with her top-secret clearance it was a no-go, which she understood and appreciated. But the things he could tell her were always toned down, especially the part he played in executing the operations.

Magic wasn't just a quiet professional, he was a humble one.

"If you say so." She let that conversation go in favor of something more exciting. "We're moving in together."

"Yeah," Magic whispered and brushed his lips over her cheek.

Gah.

See? Totally sweet.

"I think we should celebrate."

"Why do I feel like my sweet Stella has something naughty in mind?"

"Because you know me?"

"Right." He chuckled. "Or it could be the fact you're squirming on my lap."

"I'm trying to get comfy."

"Or you could be—"

Stella slapped her hand over his mouth and narrowed her eyes. "If you say horny one more time, I swear I'm taping your mouth shut."

Magic mumbled something unintelligible from behind her hand, then kissed her palm before he peeled it away. "First, you wouldn't tape my mouth shut because you know how much I like to use it on you. Second, you wouldn't tape it shut because you like the way I use it. Third, I was going to ask if you were ready for me to use it now because I'm really fucking hungry."

Stella shivered and wiggled on his lap at the thought of all the places he liked to use his mouth on her. However, he was wrong about one thing—she didn't like the way he used it, she *loved* it. Next thing she knew, she was on her back, the sheets tangled between her legs, and Magic was going for her sweats.

"No fair," she mock-frowned. "It's my turn."

"It sure as fuck is," he said and tossed her pants over his shoulder.

"I get to taste you first this time."

"Nope. Rule is, you always go first."

"Magic!"

"Stella."

"Am I really begging you to let me suck you off?" she huffed, and Magic gifted her with the best Valentine's Day gift ever. He dropped his head to her chest and roared with laughter. That meant she felt it in two places—straight to her heart and deep in her soul. Well, three actually, if you counted the clit throb the vibration caused. All of that was wonderful.

But the best gift was that of compromise.

Magic brought her up to her knees, rolled to his back, and positioned his mouth *right there*. Her whole body wracked with the be-all and end-all tremble when she understood what was going to happen. His hands gripped her hips and pulled her down. It was then Stella learned the true meaning of tongue fucking, and her man was damn good at it. Just as Stella was damn good with hers.

It was not a day she'd tell their children about, but years later, she would tell the story about how a man caught her when she fell out of a tree. She'd go on to tell the story about how he'd protected her. It was not a long tale, it didn't take hours to tell. It was short and sweet, full of love and laughter.

And sex. Lots and lots of sex, but the naughty bits she'd keep between her and Magic.

EPILOGUE

"You nervous?" Magic asked Dash as they made their way into the building where Stella and Holly worked.

"Nope."

No, his friend wouldn't be. The last year had been damn good. Holly had moved in with Dash, and Stella had found a house to rent not too far from their friends, which worked out well when he and Dash got called away on a mission. The women were close, they got together frequently, which made his leaving a little easier. Okay, that was a bald-faced lie—he hated leaving Stella—but she handled it like a pro. And according to Dash, Holly, being independent, had taken his absence the same way Stella took his—in stride.

"By the way, you totally owe me for putting on the uniform," Magic grouched.

"Lying bastard. Stella loves you in your dress greens."

Dash wasn't wrong. The few times he'd had to wear his dress uniform in the last year had led to some kinky role play. One couldn't say that Stella didn't have a wild side. And in the last year, their attraction hadn't diminished. If anything, their need had grown. It wasn't about sex, it was about closeness and intimacy. Two things Magic hadn't known he was missing. Stella made him happy in a way he never knew he could be. She brightened everything.

"You'll be back in time, right?" Dash asked as they entered the office.

Okay, so maybe Dash was a little nervous.

"We wouldn't miss it."

"Yet, I'm missing yours," his friend complained.

"Enjoy this. Let Holly enjoy it. Three days from now, she's gonna be walking toward you. In a few months, Stella and I will have a big celebration."

The women came into view, and everything about Dash's demeanor changed. Gone was his battle buddy, the hardened warrior who fought beside him. And in his place was a man in love. Magic knew the feeling, totally understood the transformation—he felt it, too. As soon as Stella was near, everything settled. A peace washed over him. She was truly the woman of his dreams.

As the men approached, the women stopped whispering and Stella turned to face him. God, she was beautiful. Head-to-toe stunning. But her true beauty came from within.

Out of the corner of his eye, he saw Dash hand Holly her bouquet of roses. There was chatter but it turned into white noise when Stella smiled at him.

"My sweet Stella," he greeted. "Ready?"

"Beyond ready."

"We better hit the road."

Impatient as ever, Dash was already pulling Holly toward the front door. Stella's giggle brought his attention back to her.

"Boy, he's in a hurry," she whispered, then dropped her voice even lower. "She has no idea."

Yeah, well, Stella didn't know everything either.

"Good. He wants it to be a surprise."

Stella gave him a wink and a blinding smile. She was thrilled for her friend.

"Was it painful keeping the secret?"

"Yes. Especially when she was asking my opinion on what you guys had planned. I wanted to tell her about it yesterday so bad, but I didn't. And it sucks I couldn't wear my ring into work..." She paused and gave him big eyes. "My ring. Please tell me you grabbed it off the nightstand. If not, we have to go back. I'm not going the entire weekend without—"

"Relax. I have it, and our bags are in the truck. Now all we have to do is get to the airport before we miss our flight."

Dash and Holly were almost to the door when Holly craned her neck and looked back at Stella. Stella returned the look with wide eyes. One of her brows lifted and he knew the women were in the midst of silent communication. This had also not changed. The two of them could have an entire conversation without words.

As they made their way outside, Stella was vibrating with excitement. Sure she was happy for her best friend and the surprise she knew Holly was in store for, but Magic was pleased to know her enthusiasm was for them.

"Ring," she clipped as soon as Holly was far enough away.

Magic pulled the engagement ring from his pocket, and just like he'd done the night before when he asked her to marry him, he slid the diamond on her finger, brought it up to his lips, and kissed it.

"I love when you do that." Soft words from his sweet girl.

"I just plain love you."

"We're going to Vegas to celebrate our engagement." She bounced from toe to toe.

Sure they were; that was the story and he was sticking to it...right up until the surprise.

"Call me later," Stella shouted to Holly.

"I will," her friend yelled back before disappearing into Dash's car.

"You just couldn't help yourself could you?"

"Well, I had to play it off like I don't know Dash is gonna ask my best friend in the whole world to marry him tonight. And like I don't know that she'll be Mrs. Dash in a few days."

Magic helped her into the truck, and he did it laughing. "Still can't pronounce his last name, can you?"

"I speak five languages," she deadpanned.

"Yet...you still can't pronounce Anagnostopoulos."

"It's fifteen letters, Magic. I don't speak Greek."

"Neither do I baby, yet I can say it."

"Whatever," she grumbled and his body shook with laughter.

"I love it when you laugh."

No games. Not then, not now.

Goddamn, he loved her.

———

"Oh my God. I love it here."

Stella had said that no less than ten times since they'd dropped their bags in the hotel room and hit the strip. The first time she stopped was outside the Bellagio to check out the fountains, then she'd turned and looked across the street and gasped when she saw the Eiffel Tower in front of the Paris. Tomorrow night they had tickets to go up to the viewing deck, not that Stella knew that.

They'd barely made it a block before she'd stopped them so she could take in Caesar's Palace, and she'd skipped across the overpass and took a million pictures including a selfie of them in front of the Flamingo.

Even though they had an appointment at the Venetian—not that she knew they were in a hurry— Magic didn't have the heart to rush her. She was glowing in the bright neon lights of Sin City. The lights seemed to dance off her shiny blonde locks. Or maybe he was a man deliriously in love and was seeing shit. Either way, he was enjoying her happiness. She stopped, pointed, commented, gawked at the grandeur, but more importantly, she hadn't stopped smiling since they'd checked into the Bellagio.

His Stella was beautiful always, but right then her beauty glowed.

Thirty minutes later, with five minutes to spare,

they walked into the Venetian and Stella gasped. Not even Magic, a man not prone to gawking or gasping, could deny the opulence was breathtaking in an over-the-top, theatrical way.

"Holy wow," she breathed.

From the marble columns, painted ceilings, the gold, the patterned marble floors, "wow" about summed it up. Later, he'd walk her around the shops and casino before their gondola ride. He'd made sure they had an hour to look around before they floated around the Grand Canal.

"Magic." Stella tugged on his hand. "Look."

He was looking all right—looking at the most stunning woman he'd ever laid eyes on. And she was tugging him exactly where he needed them to go. He'd thought about waiting until they got to Vegas to propose. But when he thought about them, about Stella, his mind always went back to that damn tree. So, really, as corny as it was, it was a no-brainer. He had to ask her to marry him in the spot where she fell into his arms—and life.

She wasn't surprised. He'd told her a year ago, and even though he was one day early on that promise, she knew it was coming mostly because, over the last twelve months, he'd complained often she wasn't wearing his ring. Which thankfully she'd happily accepted.

Last Valentine's Day had been perfect. This one, however, was going to be better.

Magic pulled her to a stop in front of a gigantic red sculpture and twisted her so his front was pressed to her back. He dropped his head and brushed his lips below her ear. She shivered, though she always did.

"Marry me," he whispered.

Stella snuggled back and held up her left hand. "I already said yes." She wiggled her fingers to punctuate her reminder.

Christ, he loved hearing her say the word yes. All he needed was one more, and an I do, and he'd be the happiest man alive.

"Right now, my sweet Stella. Marry me."

"Are you serious?"

Magic pointed next to the nicely dressed woman standing next to a giant letter L, the first of the four letters in the sculpture.

"Right here, right now. I want to marry you in front of the O. That way, we can see the waterfall behind it. What do you say? Marry me? Become Mrs. Jacklin?"

"Let me go," she demanded, but didn't wait for him to release her before she wiggled herself to face him.

"Yes, yes, yes. I want to marry you right here,

right now. It's perfect. You're perfect. Best place to get married," she rushed out, then looked behind her. "I'm marrying you in front a big red sign that says LOVE."

"What do you say we do that now?"

"Two minutes," she said and faced him.

"Are you—"

"No games. You're the best thing that's ever happened to me. Every day I fall more in love with you."

Goddamn, but he loved her.

"No games. Straight-up truth. I knew I was going to marry you the day I moved into my apartment, and from my balcony, I saw you drop your keys. You cursed a blue streak without using a single cuss word. Only person I know who uses God bless America as an expletive. Then you bent forward and spilled your coffee. Two seconds later, you were laughing yourself stupid. It was right then, seeing you smile, I knew I wanted to see that for the rest of my life. I wanted to wake up to your smile, go to sleep seeing you smile, I wanted to hear it in your voice, and I wanted you to give it to my children." Magic brushed her hair from her shoulder and Stella braced for her lip touch, but he waited. "I love you, sweet Stella."

His woman got her lip brush, he got his shiver, then he got something else.

"Gah. You're so much better at that than me. What, is there like Delta poet training?"

Magic's head dipped, their foreheads touched, and he laughed loud and long. It echoed around the atrium, people stared, but he didn't give the first fuck. His sweet Stella was funny.

———

Be sure to catch Riley's brand new series, TAKE-BACK, with book 1, *Dangerous Love*.

OTHER BOOKS BY RILEY EDWARDS

The Red Team

Nightstalker

Protecting Olivia

Redeeming Violet

Recovering Ivy

Rescuing Erin

The Gold Team

Brooks

Thaddeus

Kyle

Maximus

Declan

The Blue Team

Owen

Gabe

The 707 Freedom Series

Free

Freeing Jasper

Finally Free

Freedom

The Next Generation

Saving Meadow

Chasing Honor

Finding Mercy

Claiming Tuesday

Adoring Delaney

Keeping Quinn

Taking Liberty

Standalone

Romancing Rayne

Falling for the Delta

ABOUT THE AUTHOR

Riley Edwards is a bestselling multi-genre author, wife, and military mom. Riley was born and raised in Los Angeles but now resides on the east coast with her fantastic husband and children.

Riley writes heart-stopping romance with sexy alpha heroes and even stronger heroines. Riley's favorite genres to write are romantic suspense and military romance.

Don't forget to sign up for Riley's newsletter and never miss another release, sale, or exclusive bonus material. https://www.subscribepage.com/RRsignup

Facebook Fan Group

www.rileyedwardsromance.com

facebook.com/Novelist.Riley.Edwards

twitter.com/rileyedwardsrom

instagram.com/rileyedwardsromance

bookbub.com/authors/riley-edwards

amazon.com/author/rileyedwards